T0266795

BOA
EDITIONS LTD

❧ *Jewelry Box* ❧

Jewelry Box

A Collection of Histories

AURELIE SHEEHAN

AMERICAN READER SERIES, NO. 21

BOA EDITIONS, LTD. ❧ ROCHESTER, NY ❧ 2013

For information about permission to reuse any material from this book please
contact The Permissions Company at www.permissionscompany.com or e-mail
permdude@eclipse.net.

Publications by BOA Editions, Ltd.—a not-for-profit
corporation under section 501 (c) (3) of the United States
Internal Revenue Code—are made possible with funds
from a variety of sources, including public funds from
the New York State Council on the Arts, a state agency;
the Literature Program of the National Endowment for
the Arts; the County of Monroe, NY; the Lannan Foundation for support of the Lannan Translations Selection
Series; the Mary S. Mulligan Charitable Trust; the Rochester Area Community Foundation; the Arts & Cultural
Council for Greater Rochester; the Steeple-Jack Fund;
the Ames-Amzalak Memorial Trust in memory of Henry

ART WORKS.
arts.gov

State of the Arts

NYSCA

Ames, Semon Amzalak and Dan Amzalak; and contributions from many individuals
nationwide. See Colophon on page 124 for special individual acknowledgments.

Cover Design: Sandy Knight
Interior Design and Composition: Richard Foerster

BOA Logo: Mirko

Library of Congress Cataloging-in-Publication Data

Sheehan, Aurelie, 1963–
 [Short stories. Selections]
 Jewelry box : a collection of histories / by Aurelie Sheehan. — First edition.
   p. cm.
 ISBN 978-1-938160-24-0 (pbk) -- ISBN 978-1-938160-25-7 (ebook)
 I. Title.
 PS3569.H392155A6 2013
 813'.54—dc23

2013013227

BOA Editions, Ltd.
250 North Goodman Street, Suite 306
Rochester, NY 14607
www.boaeditions.org
A. Poulin, Jr., Founder (1938–1996)

for Alexandra

Contents

The life of our city is rich in poetic and marvelous subjects. The marvelous envelops and permeates us like the atmosphere; but we don't see it.

—Charles Baudelaire

Jewelry Box

She had been in love once, or twice, or three times, and so when the moment came to open the jewelry box for her daughter, she hesitated. The box was stitched red silk, puffy and soft, padded and embroidered with flowers and leaves and birds. It was her heart: that was obvious. And when she opened the lid to all the hard, broken things, the pins and the clasps, her eyes darted back to her daughter. At that moment the fastest hands in the West were still resting like a bird on a bench.

"Will you be careful?" she asked in the tone she used to tell the child to stop throwing popcorn, or be still at the bank. The question was scripted, just a line; her anger never had any fire in it. And her concern for safety was so immense she could only whisper it.

"Yes, I'll be careful."

The rings were offered up like kissing lips, cozy coins, half-suns behind the horizon. Not uniform at all, and not really very expensive, any of them, and only one or two cherished. The bird in flight carved from white abalone, now grayed between feather cuts. Four silver hoops from a long ago wedding cake—she'd been single then, eager to collect fairy tales. A pearl ring her grandmother gave her. Nana: once vibrant, or at least fun to have lunch with. Nana, whose fingers fretted endlessly around the sweater cuff now; whose fingers, though gnarled and leathered and panic stricken, still held the peculiar shape she didn't know she knew so well until she saw it distorted but still there, really there. A silver ring from Mexico, given to her by her father after the trip he made when he met his second wife. A ring Susan said she should buy, and so she did, of course, loving Susan, though it was too big and would never fit, this love. Two rings she bought herself when she was between this and that. Other junky stuff, and a smoky topaz her mother wore, and her grandmother before that.

The little girl reaches beyond the rings and grabs a dragonfly pin, cheap metal trinket. "What's this?"

The dragonfly was made in Japan, and the colors and the head are flattened out by industry, by twenty years in the dark, by assimilation and representation. She'd always said to herself, when she wore this cheap bit, that it would be seen as it was meant to be seen, half a joke, not real jewelry, and all that was beyond the little pin, all that was promised, all the tang of the catchy wing, the blackness of the true unseeing eye, the squirt and agony of the real body, exotic, obscene, grotesque—all the plumpness and the sass and the rainbow of herself would be remarkable, obvious, in contrast.

To the girl it is just an object. She studies the gunmetal hollow belly and then puts it back.

Mardi Gras necklaces, a tangle of them, like a bird's nest. A broken pocket watch given to her by a man who did not wear watches or carry them in his pocket. A gift of a kind. Here in a red sack are her teeth—wisdom teeth. She'll not open that. She reaches for a gold bangle. "See? This is what we wore in the seventies when we were pretending to be Stevie Nicks or Joni Mitchell."

But her daughter has grabbed the red bag of teeth.

"Don't open that."

They too could be a necklace, and now here they are, in her daughter's peach palm. Four teeth. She remembers the dead white cat she'd seen on the road when she was the age her daughter is now. Protect? Invite? The girl has not yet cut herself: not on a pin, not on anything.

T-shirt

Her other T-shirt has the Adidas logo on it, and just last week she learned how to pronounce that word: rhymes roughly with make it *last*. If things last two weeks or two months it's a long time when you're fourteen, and the newness of the day overlays your life like a coat of paint, blues and blacks and reds over a suburban gesso wash.

Relax, your parents fit into a category of difficulties called *parents*.

Relax, your body is a mystery, capable of withstanding much violence, and it's called *the body*.

The T-shirt is on sale for five dollars. What a deal! Mickey Mouse doing his characteristic bashful one-foot-forward dalliance. She buys it.

Time is really very easy to understand. The teenager will strip in the hostel bedroom, a dormitory room with bunk beds. Everyone else is downstairs already, time for dinner on the wharf. She will look about two hundred times cooler in this T-shirt than she did before. She will not re- alize that she's been joined upstairs by Bruce C., the one who showed everyone the condom he had in his wallet last night, the one who wears a jean jacket, and what is it about him really? Something about him crosses a line, something sexy and also disgusting, and she's afraid of it. He will see the girl, the teenager, because he's come up to get, of all things, that same wallet—though not to fetch the crinkled-up condom package he found in his brother's room six months ago and has carried, a talisman, ever since. He'll stop in the doorway when he sees her. He'll watch her rummage in the bag and then, in one long stretching movement, take off her shirt. She's not wearing a bra, but he'll only see her from the back. Her back is white with many freckles, and she's skinny, and it will almost look like her back goes in where her spine is, not out, and that will be so odd for Bruce C., so fearful, a little like—a little like his baby sister's back, only skinnier, and then before much time has passed this new shirt will drop over her skin—white sheet of blindness—and he will remember who this girl is, the exact clique she's in, the exact relationship between them, and his eyes will shut, and he'll hold in his mind the image of her terrifying back, a back that creates a more powerful tenderness in him than a fourteen-year-old ought to be able to gin up, a back that is not a *Playboy* back or a jerk-off back or any girl's back—though it will become, in its specificity, an anonymous back—but rather is, for that second, a part of his own fingerprint, riddled with doubt and surety, the most terrifying white, freckled back, the impossible moment of skin, igniting a kind of absurd sexual appetite which comes from down there, but from somewhere else, too—and then she screams.

Duck

He is a he, has all the characteristics of a man, male of the species, lord and warrior. He is not a butterfly—though a butterfly can be male. He is not a rock—though a rock is strong and sometimes practical. The water is chopped up like mica, but with fear attached, the fear of anything that moves. The oddest fear is that of stillness, lack of change, the years passing by with no good use, no fun, no liberation. Easier and more classifiable in the fear department: blue truck coming from the left, punctured bicycle tire, punctured heart, stabbing wound from lurking outsider, ritualistic maiming of beloved living creature, sabotage of cherished object, flowering illness, arrival of an unpleasant neighbor.

The girl thinks he must be male because she thought "he" when she saw him, and because she's used to imbuing things with a gender, as if she speaks French or Spanish, which she does, but poorly. The duck can be seen in quick cuts on the other side of the rock. He is swimming, paddling with his short legs in the frigid waves. It's the time of night when everything is up for grabs, and the thing you fear happens. In the day she believes that if she identifies it, names the fear in her head, then surely it won't actually become reality, occur—for what a coincidence *that* would be.

The duck seems frightened by the rocks, and by the sea. The sky is darkening, and the clouds lean over the duck and the girl like parents, teachers who have discovered them behind the back fence, doing something. It is good and right to have teachers, parents, even if they are didactic and strange. It is good and right to feel in the fold of something powerful. You can hear the repeating waves lapping faster and faster and without regard to sequence or shape or order against the pilings. The girl kneels on the black boulder and leans further out, to the sea.

Story

Some days it seems I have a lot to say, that life holds important and beautiful stories. Other days, life isn't shaped like that—into stories and whatnot. Some of those other times I feel, you know, tired, lazy, nothing to say, nothing to do, no interest in anything, irritated with myself for not holding to various standards, not thin enough, don't remember enough dates in history, shouldn't have treated A or B human that way, how will I feel when they are dead, wouldn't it be nice to have a drink right now, maybe a gin and tonic, or maybe a shot of tequila, or maybe a glass of cognac in bed with the long book I'm reading at the moment—the author of which feels life when he writes, or at least it seems that way.

When I see a woman in stretch pants and a push-up bra and lots of eyeliner, I make a vague mental note to dress more like her tomorrow. Tomorrow, I'll put the effort in. So then tomorrow comes and I put on a T-shirt and jeans. (Although I do have these basketball sneakers—they're blue.)

Cocteau says you aren't free until your parents are dead, but I think the main problem is with my name. I've got to start going by Sheehan. *Sheehan says you are free even if your parents aren't dead. Sheehan says that green eyeliner and stretchy pants are the thing. And also that you don't need to have eighteen cats, or write naked, or wear all white, to be somebody.*

The problem with life is that it isn't over, that's the problem with *that* story.

What about sounds? I can do sounds. The way I sounded out *mag-nif-i-cent* when I typed it, or the beeps and wrinkles that count for words from my baby. Or my husband's voice at night, the sound of our voices together in the dark, murmurs of assent after lovemaking, like two shoppers who've found a very nice brass lamp, or two giddy senior citizens who've come upon the shrimp bowl at a buffet. I think Rushdie is good, too, and Hemingway. I think writing about sex in general would be fine, and also writing like a fucking maniac, in a café. *Sheehan writes like a fucking maniac, in a café*, sources will murmur confidentially.

AURELIE SHEEHAN

Telephone Call

The ex-lover calls on the phone. They are watching TV. She gets up off the couch when the phone rings, not in a million years thinking it will be him. Joe? When she hears the voice, she knows it's familiar and dangerous, but she's not sure who it is at all, not consciously.

Maybe inside she already remembers the way she felt on the beach, years before. Even then he was an ex-lover; even then she was taken by another (another another). It was hot and overcast and they sat at the edge of the ocean, the waves reaching up between her legs, the sand repeatedly collapsing—building and collapsing—underneath her bare legs. To begin with, she would normally be sitting on a towel, safely halfway up the beach, and second of all—

They sat on the edge of the water and he was behind her, his legs, so familiar and yet somehow inhuman to her, surrounding hers. His legs looked casual—to be damned by casual legs, casual hands, casual hair! At twenty-two, he was casual and that meant one thing, though she'd wished it meant something else, and now—now what does it mean when he's forty-four?

The water was gray like stones, but clear, and the sand was wet and gravelly and in her bikini bottom—and now here was a casual hand on her belly, on the cloth of her bikini, on the inside of her thigh, the very white place where secrets live—and healthy families were eating snacks and listening to the radio just over there—

And people were walking by—just here—and here—

His hand. And the waves, the sand, the damnable bright day—if there were only a tent, a quiet towel, a bed with pure white cotton sheets nearby—it was almost as if the world were shifting on its axis. She couldn't see straight.

Is this her?

Is this him, on the phone, after all these years? She has a husband and child. *I am married—I have a child!* she wants to shout when she realizes who it is on the phone. She doesn't want to listen to this, this voice. She wants to shout it down. Reorient who she is. She is not this man's lover. *I am not your lover*, she would shout, but that would cause a commotion here at home. After all, he's just speaking some kind of strange gibberish—he never actually made sense, verbally, only physically did they make any kind of sense at all—and her husband is staring at the TV, a tranquil look on his face. Doesn't he realize the danger? And the gibberish continues and then she's getting off the phone—she's looking at the polished wooden floor of her living room, where she lives with her husband and infant and three rapscallion cats, and he says, "I've always loved you, I'll always love you, I've loved you since you were fourteen years old." And she says, "Oh, that's nice. Thank you." And she wants to shout: *That doesn't make any sense! You don't know me! You don't know who I am! How did you get my number?* He lives on an island and has never had a job—it's never really been clear how he lives at all, this lunatic on the fringe of wealthy societies—Nantucket, Westport—who knows everyone and has never, not in his lifetime, ironed one of his Brooks Brothers shirts that he stores in wadded jumbles in corners.

And what about the ramifications, the responsibilities, the nuances, the chambers of love, the places it grows together? What about what she thought it once meant, and what about what she thought it meant later? Means now.

I have always loved you.

She felt his thigh, like plastic, tan unfeeling plastic, and she felt his erection, too. How she would have turned toward him and how fiercely she'd have pushed him back and stretched her legs to each side of his legs and how she would have shut his mouth with her own—

Shut his mouth with her own. *That's nice, Joe. Thank you.*

Cup of Coffee

He drank. He took a sip from the Styrofoam and hesitated. What did he think of it, we all wondered. Did it mean something? My brother, Bartleby, who never drank coffee. My brother who had to resist us all: resist my mother's encroachment, resist my father's cheer, resist my sanctimony. He spent years honing his *thank you, no*, to this family of coffee drinkers. He didn't shout and storm around like the rest of us. He seemed, in his equanimity, to be happy.

Of course, I can't publish this secret.

Didn't Dad write about a mute boy?

Didn't Mom tell him he ought to make money?

The family dynamic needs to be honored. So I will change his name, or his sex; perhaps I will make his parents Russian peasantry.

Shoes

They were very trampy. Very very *very* trampy. The thrill didn't happen through the glass, no, but it was there when she walked in, up to the whorish, slutty shoes.

Oh, look at them.

She looked to her left and right to see if she was alone. On the subway, three men had come close to her before she knew it, and she'd felt the thrill and exhaustion of fear, the yellow trickle of it, the way your muscles weaken, liquidate, the shaking of her fingers as she fiddled with her purse, pretending to be secure.

In her dream world, she'd have all black or white clothing, plus a handful of long, strangling scarves in purple, crimson, azure, and ochre.

The shoes were illuminated on a clear plastic shelf. Behind them, a white slatted wall.

Where did the spotlight come from? The needling little beam that emanated from nowhere, everywhere.

She didn't need shoes. Of course not, who did?

What happened to all her old shoes? She'd had shoes of every description, a smutty, nasty pair like these, and then boots that hid in the corner.

Sometimes hiding is sexy, the scholar said. His discourse had been so dull she'd fallen asleep for sweet bitter moments in the uncomfortable auditorium chair. She'd considered writing some of it down, to try out later, but she'd been too bored or tired, and besides, she couldn't remember his phrases soon after they'd appeared. Could a sound appear? Would the scholar think the appearance of a sound was sexy? Perhaps he would. Perhaps, magnanimously, they were. Was he very *very* good in bed, this scholar? Would he take his hat off, then rest it carefully on the bedside table?

The classmates shut their eyes in mockery when he pulled out the tribal audiotape. They pretended to be where the drum was, but the drum wasn't there—the drum was a lie to these people—these people none of whom had shoes as sexy as these.

She would touch the shoes, but she'd wait.

Drifting around the store, she was the girl she'd been on the playground about a million years ago—rebuffed and enacting her own elaborate and whispery drama. She was the girl she'd been ten minutes ago on the subway.

A Liar and Her Brother

Well, I wanted to tell you a little more about Donna's family. It was the mother, in this case, who was the alcoholic. Donna would recount, with that classic simper, how she'd come home from school to find her mother crumpled at the bottom of the stairs. Then Donna would push the lighter in the dashboard of her ugly car and hold it there, wobbling it with one pink chapped finger, until the curl turned orange.

When Donna smoked, it was with the gestures of someone who had been smoking forever in front of a trailer home, or in the front office of a trucking company. She was grown up differently than we were. She never tried anything new with her hair (straight blond) or her makeup, and she wrote in red pen and she smoked Mores. She was still smoking Mores at a restaurant in New York City a few years later when I met her for lunch and she let out such a fascinating compendium of lies that she must have known that I knew, didn't she? To my knowledge, I had never met a compulsive liar before.

I went to the senior prom with her brother, Josh, who went on to Harvard for three and a half years, and then dropped out and began living in a boiler room under a Cambridge office building. He gave my best friend all his wisdom teeth as a gift one night—he taped the baggie to her bedroom window. He didn't want any presents that Christmas, and instead asked his parents to send money to Save the Children, an unprecedented act of selflessness in high school. Before the prom, we were all meeting at Mia and Ryan's house for dinner. We were going to grill steaks. The boys brought the beef for their girls. Josh unwrapped his white-papered package and showed us what he'd brought. It was a minute steak. My date had brought a minute steak. Everyone laughed at him then, just another sign that he was off his rocker. He grinned, too. We drank our forbidden beers and hobbled around for a while in taffeta and polyester.

Suntan Lotion

She notices how small his feet are and wonders if a man can be strong and still have small feet. Does her father have small feet? Does her mother? The feet, small as they are, move back and forth awkwardly as he reaches behind him into the cooler. It's as if they have a life of their own, or maybe that they have no life at all.

"Budweiser or—looks like there's one more Corona."

"I'll take the Corona," she says. What else is there? The afternoon is entirely lost.

He's facing forward again. When he faces forward, his feet disappear and are replaced by his frightening eyes, looking up at her from above teetering sunglasses. He has a sunburned nose.

"Can you do me a favor?" she says quickly—then wishes she hadn't spoken at all.

"What's that, babe?"

She remembers that her boom box is still in his car and there is no way she can leave without it. Or she could, but her imagination isn't strong enough.

"Can you put lotion on my back?" It was late at night, just last night, when she met him, although he claimed to have seen her before. He is in the telecommunications industry and this is 1980, when even the word "telecommunications" is new and reminds her of billboards, or adding machines, or whatever. She hasn't had a date since Jonathan, and last night, she remembers, Jonathan seemed like forever ago, although at seventeen it isn't forever, exactly, only a matter of days, a month at most. No years besides this one matter in terms of what she knows, who she is, what she has learned about men as she's gotten older.

"Don't you remember, we stood by the bleachers? You were pretty messed up. A little party animal, aren't you?"

"Me? But I don't remember you. I hardly ever go to football games."

"Bet you'd look cute in a little pompom dress or whatever you call 'em."

She turned away then.

With sudden energy, he said, "Look at that asshole try to open that with his teeth. What an *asshole*!"

She looked over to the guys standing around the keg waiting for new beer. She laughed some.

He took her by the shoulder, a kind of buddy-buddy thing, a way of touching that didn't mean anything.

Now she lies on the beach, belly to the ground. The bumps are hard as boulders—wasn't sand soft, wasn't that the thing? The sun in her eye is like a shout, like her mother shouting at her about her job, or about her hair, or about her father, or about the applications to college scattered across the dining room table. She can, in the background, hear the small waves piddle against the shore, and she can hear the cars passing—cars going twenty miles an hour somewhere, away from here. He is shaking the bottle of sunscreen. Who shakes sunscreen, she wonders.

She hears the cap flip up and he leans close to her ear. She smells his cigarettes, and something else, like car freshener.

"Do you want a little—here?"

His hand passes down over her ass and he slides his fingers between her thighs. Speechless, she widens them just a little.

Rage

I was born with one limb, arm of sadness. This world creates many opportunities for me: there is walking down the gray hall, listing, looking at the concrete as if it's a window. There is lying on my side with my fist under the pillow, night gone rampant. There is that sticky place between talking and not talking: words dressed up as snowmen or wildebeests. Or there is the ever-present murmur: words coming from a place within a mouse house behind my teeth, as opposed to from my lungs or all those canyons voice instructors point toward. There is the everlasting optimism, the lack of discretion. There is a softness that surrounds me like a scarf, opening and revealing.

Others have rage within them, not attached prosthetically but as an aspect of themselves. They are good at what they do. I can watch them at restaurants and I've seen it in movies and I've seen it in real life.

Rage.

Even the sound of it knocks me over, red velvet wind sonorous and spontaneous and—

Could I put it in a little shell? Could I put it in my change purse, snap it shut and save it to spend later? I could listen to it whirl in the evening. I could learn from it.

Could I coax it out from under the bed with some dried fish treats? I could practice saying *I AM somebody.*

Rage. I could grow to love you, and we could breathe together, and we could, on a Saturday, break some things. Do not be the kind of rage that is warranted. Do not be an imbecile.

AURELIE SHEEHAN

Sexual Fantasy

When making love, sometimes she thinks of elephants. Sometimes the elephants are watching her touch herself, sometimes they are herding her into a stand of palm trees and she can feel the pressure of the tree against her stomach, and she can feel the elephant against her ass and thighs. Usually these elephants are quite large, even for elephants, and they are unknown to her. Sometimes she thinks of a certain subspecies of elephant of which there is only one. Or sometimes she thinks of elephants with ears that are frilled at the edges, and the frills shudder in the wind of their excitement together, and she can keep fixed on that sight: the sight of the shuddering pink-gray ear, and all she wants to do is touch it.

Sometimes there are two elephants. It's hard to see their faces, but they are stern and forceful elephants. But they are not criminal or bad elephants. But they are much bigger than she is and they *will* have their way, being elephants.

Often the elephant undresses her in a haphazard fashion: he may pull aside something, ripping it, and he doesn't care, and she doesn't care, because he is into his own elephant mythology and she only hopes that he will finish what he has started.

Sometimes she dreams about cheetahs, too. Cheetahs in addition to elephants, usually, but sometimes only cheetahs. The cheetahs are long and their fur is frantic with something like music, some kind of reflection that comes from rivers, the hue of their spots that changes when they move, always revealing some other aspect. She herself is more like a cheetah. When she dreams of the cheetahs, she sometimes gets confused in the dream and realizes she doesn't know if she is doing, or being done to. She finds the flank of the cheetah extraordinary. There is a synergy between the tense muscle and the flab of skin, and the bone. She keeps focused on this. It's like flipping through a book of images, but each image is the same: the flank, its velvet fur, its anxiety, its quiver, and then the flank again, and the flank, and the flank.

Sometimes her tongue on the flank.

She is almost always in no position to negotiate with these animals: either her desire is so strong that she begs them to use her, or their desire is so strong that they steamroll over any doubts she might have, any thoughts about tea leaves or the mending of her butterfly net.

Both or all three of them are always in the vortex. It's fate, without morals or afterthoughts or family histories or hardly even personalities. It's all about reaching the edge and then going further.

Sometimes when she is being pushed by the elephant against the sink, or the bar, or the wall, or against the ground, he remarks to another elephant that she is ready. Sometimes when she is with the cheetah, and she is bringing the cheetah toward the vortex, and she is likewise compelled toward the vortex by the cheetah, the elephant has been watching, and the elephant must come to them.

Sometimes she imagines herself at the last place she actually saw the elephant in real life. Just the location has a charge.

There is an amount of society, an amount of psychology. And there are the images: the flank, and, of course, the curve of the elephant's trunk, and the sense of unyielding.

It all spins in her head, and she is not sure what it means, what it says about her, but it brings her to the place she wants to go.

And yet, these are only things that represent other things. They are unreal. They are as real as this page.

Mascara

She showered. She used the shampoo that smelled like bub-
ble gum, but was really an exotic combination of rosemary
and mint, and she used the conditioner that went with it.
She used nectarine soap. She lathered her body with it carefully. And then she scrubbed herself with a puff of plastic.
And then she shaved her legs, all the way up the leg, back
and front, and her armpits. And then she dried off. And
then she sprayed some other conditioner/detangler on her
hair. And then she clipped her fingernails and filed them.
And then she spread face moisturizer on her face and then
she rubbed body moisturizer over the rest of her body.
And then she combed her hair. And then she put special
moisturizing cream on her feet. And then she tweezed her
eyebrows and the one stray hair under her chin. And then
she cleaned her ears with a Q-tip. And then she brushed
her teeth. And then she used mouthwash. And then she
flossed. And then she put on her underpants and bra. And
then she rubbed a cream of some kind into her hair and
started blow-drying it. It took a long time to dry, as she
dried it thoroughly, and as she had two different brushes
she used, a round one and a flat one. And when it was dry
she combed a part in her hair. And then she sprayed something else in her hair. And then she put on a blouse and
shorts. And then she stood by the mirror and placed her
makeup bag on the sink, behind the faucets. And then she
sloughed her skin. And then she applied foundation to her
skin. And then she applied eye shadow to her eyelids. And

then she applied eyeliner to her eyelids. And then she applied mascara to her eyelashes. And then she applied blush to her cheeks. And then she applied concealer under her eyes. And then she applied sparkly gel around her eyes. And then she applied lip pencil. And then she applied lipstick. And then she applied perfume. And then she brushed her hair a little more. And then she smoothed her hand over her leg. And then she applied a little more moisturizing cream to her elbows, knees, and her feet again. And then she inspected her toes. And then she noted that her nail polish had chipped. And then she dabbed nail polish on two toenails. And then she put on her sandals. And then she looked in the full-length mirror. And then she turned to the side to look from a different angle. And then she realized she had forgotten to weigh herself, so she took off her sandals and weighed herself. And then she put her sandals back on and looked back in the mirror, one side, other side, front. And then she picked up her sunglasses. And then she put them on and looked in the mirror. And then she put them up on her head and looked in the mirror. And then she shrugged. And then she picked up her car keys and her purse. And then she went to him.

House

No one owned the house, or, it could be said, no one that mattered. But the house did believe in herself. For instance: she believed in her location. She sat on a foundation between the 20th and 21st centuries, between Arlington and Alexandria, between 4246 and 4250, between owners—

—is it good, is it right, to be owned? Owners were so self-righteous, their snobbism so ingrained—you could call it, above all, an assumption. The woman might twirl around in the cool living room, all gleaming wood floor and white wall, and say: "All this is mine," or "This is *so* us!" And soon enough she'd place, in the crook of your arm, a cranky old television and your peace was over. They came to inhabit you, these people, with their locks and their papers. It wasn't enough that they named you—4248, or sometimes even Sporthill Manor, Butlerstown House, Bear River Farm, Regency Place—but then they drilled holes into your face and put up a sign. You became something specific to them then, when the naming was over.

Although it was true, the house knew the desire to start anew. Not as the vassal or vessel of someone fresh, not that— the house wanted time to be alone and think about what it meant to be her. *Her* long walls. *Her* flat floors. *Her* cabinets and closets to keep secret winds and gullies. *She* wanted to do the remembering, in-house as it were.

It was evening, and 4246 was thumping up the stairs and 4250 had permitted the application of some sort of lacquer.

She had seen art. She had seen biology. Botany, politics, nursing, teaching, kissing, lovemaking, pining, fighting—her walls trembled with feeling. But if she shook, they called in a plumber. Or they shut their eyes, believing a ghost lived here.

She tightened all her braces and joints and shingles; she tightened, squeezed, and all went dark, darker—and then she let all the stories she knew jumble into a whirl of stars and blood, all the things that don't last or illuminate. If the assessor (like a dog catcher) had come then, she'd have been one half-inch wider.

Yes, the house said, she was an accumulation of all that had happened here (and the sweet holly and the cardinal, and the pansy and the crow). But at times she let go of what she knew. And this is how they loved her, how they captured her: white-walled and quiet. How far down could she go? Would remembering and unremembering get harder as she grew older? Would she by mistake let the odor of one evening escape into another, twenty years newer?

How could she keep vigilant enough to be slave to their desires?

It would be easy. They would knock, and if she were alone, she'd open the door.

Letters

He was legendary in his own way, like all grandfathers. He lived at a country club in Chicago, part of a fading aristocracy. We'd fly out to visit every summer.

The country club's driveway was lined with white pillars, and the lake beach had a snack bar where I bought Three Musketeers bars, and a screen door that slapped shut the way only screen doors can in a nine-year-old's summer. The grown-ups would meet up with me and my brother and my mother, or whoever was taking care of us, before their golf round and after tennis, at the Bird Cage, the "casual" restaurant with big fans and grilled cheese and tomato sandwiches—stunning novelty! And then there was the fancy restaurant, at the far end of the lobby, a long room set up with a row of sitting areas, brocade furniture and gleaming tables and chandeliers—and silver bowls of wafer mints in pastel pink, green, yellow, and white. It was here we ate dinner, and afterwards we'd all order Grandpa's favorite dessert, a "snowball," one scoop of vanilla ice cream rolled in coconut flakes and drizzled with chocolate sauce. It was here, somewhere between stolen mints and snowballs, that I learned manners.

But outside of manners, sometimes by myself, I'd slip away and go to the stable down the driveway, a dark precise society I could step into with impunity. Stalls lined two long walls, and the vast middle was a riding ring, thick and soft with brown peat. I knew the people here by looks. I knew the tall man in the derby hat, the nice lady I saw in the locker room. I'd walk around the ring once, twice, three times, looking in through grates to the horse in each stall, and then coaxing him toward me, a lifted nose, a caught eye, whispers.

Sometimes the horses were tied up on either side of the walkway, young women massaging them in slow circles with curry combs, petting them with soft brushes, combing or braiding their manes or tails, picking their feet clean or swabbing their hooves with conditioner. I'd dip under the rope, lurk. If they'd let me, these girls, I'd feed their horses sugar cubes—and then it was back to my mission, the full circumference of the barn, once, sometimes twice, "Diamond Girl" by Seals & Crofts playing on the radio, sung softly by myself.

That summer I took riding lessons, something my grandfather had arranged, on a horse called Blue Moon. He was a small black and white pony, the perfect size for me, with a long black mane and forelock, and a docile disposition. Once Grandpa also found a way for me to ride a five-gaited show horse like my mother and aunt used to ride when they were young. I could barely control him, but the ride was exhilarating.

One afternoon at the Bird Cage all the adults were exchanging strange, silent looks, and finally it came out: Blue Moon was sick and would be put down.

I visited the stable that day, saw him standing in the ring with some people—maybe the people who owned him. He was far away from me then, far away already, and it was unjust, to say the least, what was happening to him.

Grandpa was a fierce, apparently wealthy man, with strong feelings about manners, about adhering to the rules

of tennis and golf, and about what constituted a worth-
while meal or dessert. His face and hands were marked
with brown spots, and he had thin white hair and a gently bobbing head, as he drank his blackberry brandy, as he
smoked his single, after-dinner cigarette. Every Christmas he took us clothes shopping. At the Bird Cage the next
afternoon, he offered to buy me the fast five-gaited horse,
but I suppose that wasn't a serious offer, or at least my parents didn't take it that way. We flew home, and, in a murky
parallel world, Blue Moon was put down. Around that same
time I got the first of Grandpa's letters, typed on onion-
skin paper, describing the adventures of a little girl and a
horse called Blue Moon.

I wish I knew where those letters went. I imagine they
are buried under a pile of sweaters somewhere, or have been
thrown out in error, or have molded and disintegrated
into nothing. I still think of them as a promise, evidence
of goodwill and immortality.

Bra

I've got breasts that are like, well, champagne glasses (not flutes, the other kind). At least that's how my friend and I came to refer to them after reading in one of her father's *Playboy* magazines an article describing small breasts, the glory of them, and the perfection of the "champagne-glass size" breast. Lying belly-down on her parents' king-size bed, we mutually formed the mental image of champagne glasses cupping our own breasts, just one of many activities at a black lace and disco festivity of some fantastical kind.

Photograph

At the time of the photograph, one woman was having marital difficulties and the other wasn't married and never had been. Though the unmarried one was on the whole helpful during their conversations, not presupposing, she looked at marriage as something that you measured in years, that if you were at the kitchen table and it felt like your head was about to blow off, you could get through it by imagining the calendar, how time passes. Suddenly you're having a third or tenth anniversary. The dishes are done, everyone sleeps deeply, and the gold band shines on.

Pretty newly out of college back then, they'd switch off calls—both broke, both counting pennies. Two years before, the unmarried one had ridden to her friend's wedding on the back of a motorcycle, profoundly hungover. It seemed like her friend was doing something, well, boring. Marriage? A wedding? Her friend was the one who smoked Camel straights and drank bourbon. Her friend didn't know how to cook a thing. She drove a truck with New Mexico plates and owned a dog with a bandana tied around his neck. Now this woman was joking with her soon-to-be husband about appliances. On the back of the motorcycle, feeling briefly held up by the wind, not at this exact moment nauseous, the unmarried one had thought mostly, *no*. I don't want to get married. Not now, not him.

In the photograph, the two women are linked arm in arm. You can see the married one's knobby knees and long arms. The unmarried one wears a porkpie hat; she looks like Dennis the Menace. Each woman's hands are clasped in her lap, jumpy but strong.

It was the year the married one had developed a passion for gardening. She bought a fierce amount of bulbs and pruned and dug until dark. The feeling of the cold spade and the smell of the soil, the terrain and the map that you see, like the map that might illustrate some old-fashioned adventure tale, from here to there, a star and an arrow, a treasure over the hill. It was like that: these paths, these journeys that lizards might take, that your hands, ageless, could take in the garden. And when dusk finally fell and a chill came on, she looked up between the trees, just now blurring their bones with new foliage, and saw the charcoal streaks and the blanched color underneath, and her happiness came.

Her husband was inside at that moment, making a pie. No one knows the inside of a marriage—even, or especially, a good one. The photographic paper was hard to read by then, in the dark, no lights on. Marriage, death, birth, geography. It's all harmless, really. Everything can be folded into a drawer; everything is quiet as a caterpillar under a leaf in the garden.

Daughter

Joelle woke up one morning and realized that she had become her mother. At first it wasn't entirely clear that this was the case. She opened her eyes and saw a room, very much like her bedroom, but the walls were closer. The sun that normally woke her in the morning, a quiet expansion, today felt like a flashlight, someone trying to find her eyes in a darkened room.

She looked at her arms, long and frightful. The familiarity of maternal embraces, the capable beauty of them. These were her arms now.

But can you be a mother without a child? This realization dawned on her with something like horror; if she were a mother, she had forgotten, or misplaced, or had no idea where her responsibility lay.

Grain of Sand

The day has gotten away from me. It has drained out, and I am drained with it, and it's not just the day, it's all the days up until now, and the prospect of the days to come. I leach energy from what I see, but today I see nothing. True, there's a pomegranate hanging like lust from that tree, but I know that, most likely, I'll never pluck it from the branch and that it will die.

I am writing a review of what I am writing as I write it. I am taking a stand outside of myself, like an insect watching. I am shivering with self-recognition. I am loud, even as I sit here alone in my room. I am nowhere else. I am here. The people I know scream. Everything is quiet and seductive. I can relax. I am seeking existence. I have nothing to say.

As we become older, we gravitate toward church, not out of fear, but out of the obvious—there's less to us, physically, and our heads feel swollen with reportage and expressed feelings. Why not quietly take the slide into sheer nothingness. A grain of sand is small, but it is not nothing.

Book

My book is pink and tan and Dad reads it to me. It had once been my mother's; she wrote her name on the first blank page. When he reads I close my eyes, or sometimes I look at the pictures. Always I listen to his voice, a boat carrying me along. The river has fast and slow spots, we tip right and left and it can't last forever, something will end. Maybe the story, maybe the chapter, and it will be time to go to bed.

In the dark I close my eyes again, the voice of my father carrying the words. The pictures in the pink and tan book become my own dream. Tumbling down the hole. Seeing the shelves—the marmalade especially. Seeing the white rabbit. Seeing the key. Having a very long neck. I gather these images to me, and they are what I am inside when I walk out into the world.

One day I walk into the world and there is sex in it, and at approximately the same time maliciousness and a little violence. I stop on the sidewalk and scrutinize. This ranting, it's a bit Mad-Hatter-like. It doesn't fully make sense, and there's a kind of meanness in it. There's a trembling to the earth—no, to the back of the little mouse, the scapegoat, and there's a gratitude a person can feel to be, at least, not that one, and to feel, at least, that one is on one's own two feet, an observer. There's a moment when the observer becomes crystallized. I will allow the Mad Hatter to keep speaking, I will accompany drunkards and seek drunkards and sit smiling at trembling tables with drunkards—drunkard is only one word for it, but it is the

word on the back of the card, it's a secret word that can be
a clue, that can be read—I will allow it to go on, and I will
let his dark words come to me and destroy years at a time
and I will tend to believe what he is saying. I will run, and
be small and then big, and I will believe it's all right for a
while because although I cannot see the whole story, at least
I am embodying something familiar, for the speed makes
my head very small and the acid makes my head very big
and the cocaine, well, it makes me hard inside and the pot
makes me soft. It's not drugs, but drugs are a good start, a
template, a showy way to describe the vise around my head,
or the loose attribution of life to unlikely circumstances, to
strange houses where you speak from your place on a couch
that holds you down, to strange parties where ventriloquists
attempt to seduce you through the speech of puppets, to
strange streets where cars pull over, or to strange rivers
where hands come—I will wear a petticoat and a charming
blue ruffled dress and I will always have long blond hair
pulled back in a big blue bow, even when things are dis-
arming, such as these times, as described, or in the tread-
ing from one place to another, the steps between chapters,
between the howl of the caterpillar and the disappearing
smile, a tentative sense that there will be another adventure, that I will in any case attempt a certain uprightness,
a certain propriety, even as I lay near the young stranger
with the broken tooth in the hayloft, or as I slip a valentine
under the door with vain hope. It has felt like a dream. It
has felt like I wrote the story, or that it was written for me,
not Alice, no Alice, I'm Alice. And so there is no use in
dissembling. When I sit here and look up, the cat talks to
me and when I sit here I am scolded and when I sit here the

house becomes much too small indeed. Always the Mock Turtle is crying, and the Jabberwocky is jabbering, and always the Queen is saying *off with her head* and somewhere in the distance, soft and persistent like the rocking motion of a boat, is my father's voice, an alternate tumble, a place I can lean, guiding me through the night.

AURELIE SHEEHAN

Age at Which You Consider History

It used to be that stories remained still. Your mother or father might say them, and they were small presents, like coffee mugs or key chains. This is the ceramic sphere that I call my grandmother's response to her daughter's teen-age pregnancy. This is the plastic orb that I call the uncle who was once a baseball player and then became someone who wore gold jewelry. It used to be also that you were definitely on a surfboard all the time and it was pretty great (although also sometimes pretty terrible). You adjusted to the shivers and the shoves underneath you; you kept your eyes closed and anticipated with all your might. Whatever you did, the rude splash awoke you, devastated you, before it turned away again.

Car Ride

"Mommy do cactuses have mommies?"

"No, they don't. They just grow by themselves."

"Why?"

I am thirty-eight years old. I know the reason why I feel so anxious is because I have to tell my mother that I won't be visiting her this summer.

"Okay, so this is what I was trying to tell you in the kitchen. This guy, Dylan Biggs, he used to play for L.A., right? But they traded him. That was in the 1980s. 1988. No. 1989. Anyway—"

"That's just the way plants are. They just grow in the ground and get big. Okay, Dylan Biggs?"

"Why?"

"So they traded him to Chicago. He did fine in Chicago, but he always wanted to go back to California—one of those guys who—"

"Why, Mommy, why?"

"Plants come from seeds. In a way, they have mommies because the seeds come from another plant, and that's how they start. The little seed starts in the ground. I think that's how cactuses start."

"He really wanted to play for his home state."

"But who are the cactuses' mommies?"

Why does this affect me so much? It's April, for God's sake.

"Well, they don't really have mommies. They come from seeds."

"He was a great player back then. Amazing."

"Why?"

"That's just how plants are."

I don't even have to tell her for a month, and I'll be seeing her again in August, anyway.

"Is that a baby cactus?"

"It's rare these days and it's probably a terrible career move, but anyway, he had this conviction. So, okay, many years later he's traded back to L.A. He goes, even though he has to take a salary cut of like a million dollars."

It's her deal, this whole see-each-other-every-four-months thing. I never really agreed to it.

"Why is it a baby cactus?"

"I guess 'cause it's so little."

"Where's its mommy?"

"A million dollars? Did you get that?"

"It doesn't have a mommy. Yes, go on."

I have accommodated, to be nice. But I won't get any credit for that at all.

"Why?"

"Here's the interesting part. So he goes back there, and he just does terribly. I mean, it's like he can't even keep his hands on the ball. He drops the ball all the time. He can't make a basket to save his life."

She's going to take it personally. She always takes it personally.

"Well, it lives by itself."

"Is it lonely?"

"So, just listen to this. The guy looks like a complete clown. Pretty soon the fans in L.A. are chanting Bigg Loser whenever he shows up. The coach benches him. Then his wife leaves him."

"Wow—The cactus might be lonely, honey, but maybe it has some friends. Look, there are other cactuses too.

Those are its friends."

Why can't I just talk to her about it like a normal person? Why does it have to bother me this long?

"Then he gets some kind of terrible knee injury and he can't play anyway for a year. By then, his contract is over and he quits basketball and begins a new life—get this—bowling."

I can't let it ruin my whole summer. At this rate, I may as well go see her. It's just a few days, just a few hundred dollars. But we don't have the money and I'd really like some time for myself. Why do I rationalize it away like this? Maybe I should just call her today and tell her. Get it over with.

"Are you listening?"

"Of course."

"Are the other cactuses sad?"

It makes me sick to my stomach to do it. Do it now. Just do it. No, I should wait—maybe I'll come to some solution, at least a better psychological space about it. I'm like a moth attracted to flame. If it feels dangerous, why do I want to do it? Why not just wait?

"No, why would they be sad?"

But she's being crazy; she's got problems. It doesn't matter—she's my mother. She's a fucking control freak.

"Can you believe that? And he bowls like a crazy man. He bowls to beat the band. Okay, so there's this old man, some kind of multimillionaire bowling freak—"

Why do I have these negative feelings about my own mother? It's so awful. I'm an awful person.

"Because they have no mommies. Maybe they are lonely."

"So the old rich guy decides he wants to build a bowling hall of fame in downtown L.A. and he calls on Biggs to help him out with this."

"Yeah? But they *do* have friends, see? So it's probably okay."

I hate to think of hurting her. I'll twist myself any way I can, not to hurt her. But she gets hurt so easily, by anything. She takes everything personally. I have to look after myself sometimes. I've got a responsibility here, to myself, and to my husband and child.

"I have a mommy."

"Yes you do."

"You're my mommy."

"Yes I am."

I don't even know what my own feelings are. I wish sometimes she'd let me just get to a place where I can feel my own feelings. Feel if I do love her. I always have to resist her smothering and guilt stuff. I know I love her. I just wish I didn't have to feel so false about it, always having to resist her.

"Biggs does, and now there's the Dylan Biggs Bowling Hall of Fame right on Hollywood Boulevard, so after all that, he really did get to be part of L.A. after all."

Maybe I'll call her.

"That's amazing."

"Why?"

"Because I just am. I gave birth to you."

No, I won't.

"Oh yeah, and he gets remarried and has a couple of kids, etc., etc. Cool, right?"

"Yeah, that is."

"Why?"

"You came out of my body, and you were just a little baby."

I have to get it out of my mind for a while. It's only April. I could keep it out of my mind for a whole month.

"I was a little baby."

"Yes you were."

"But now I'm a big girl."

"Yes you are. You are three."

"I am three. Why am I three?"

"Because you turned three. Remember? You had a birthday."

"Will I have another birthday?"

"Yes you will. Someday you'll turn four. But that won't be for a while."

"Why?"

"Because people only have birthdays once a year."

"Why?"

"Well, that's just what birthdays are."

"Why?"

"What do you think? Pretty amazing, right?"

Her husband looks at her in the rear view mirror. She smiles. "Right. Definitely."

Hair

It was a regular party except none of your friends had hair.
It was a regular plane arrival, but when your mother got
there she had no hair. It was like always, making love to
your husband, except he had no hair, not on his head, or
chest, or arms, or down there. Down the street—no hair on
anyone's head, and their bodies didn't look so much like
human forms as they did absences of something, white and
black cutouts from the landscape, and you had to squint to
put the scene back together. The clerk at the store handed
you your cigarettes: his arm was like an overgrown girl's.
Waiting in the room to get the rental car: five people bald
as golf balls. They stared forward, half fixed-up manne-
quins, and you were mostly surprised by how lumpy everyone was, really, and you were mostly surprised that
flight—airborne, winged flight—seemed more urgent and
less likely than ever.

Artists

The one artist painted chickens. Cartoon chickens. Over and over, in various "hilarious" situations. One Saturday she went over to his house in her blue Pinto to clean. She was sixteen and this is what she did, she cleaned houses— ten dollars an hour. It was good money. Soon after she arrived, he asked if she'd go to the liquor store and pick up a bottle of booze for him—on the clock, of course. Well, sure, anything was better than swabbing toilets. And she could do it: she had a fake ID. Off she went to the liquor store, came back with the bottle, continued to clean. She started on his bedroom bathroom. There were girlie magazines on the floor. No big deal. The other guy she cleaned for had them too. But then something was wrong, some new sound or presence. She looked out the window. The trees were close and throbbing with insects; this was summer in Connecticut. She looked out the bathroom door to his bedroom. He was on the bed, pulling at his penis.

She retracted her head and stood in the bathroom. She thought for a second. Only one way out, and that was through the bedroom. She started walking fast, through the bedroom, down the hall, down the stairs, he was following her, she was out the door, she was at her car, she was in it, he was right behind her, scraggly beard and thin little chicken body, fucking artist, and she was rolling up the window in his face.

He wasn't the first artist she'd met. There was the man who painted nudes. Very handsome, that guy. Very. Much older than she was. She and her friend went out with him and his friend in his blue van and there was some, but not complete, sexual activity in the back of the blue van during the drive-in, and there was the return to his house. Vast canvases of naked women emerging from the ocean covering every wall. Not only the ocean. Once a meadow. He was also a very competent artist, a photorealist. The breasts of the women were rather large, their expressions breathless. She herself was a sophisticated girl. She made some comment about composition or color, as if there were no women there at all.

Those whimsical years, she also met a photographer. He came up to her and two friends at the beach. He was older, too, and certainly not the type of guy they'd even consider for boyfriend status. But he *was a* photographer. He said, in fact, that he was looking for models. He paid a hundred dollars for a half hour. All you did was take your top off, nothing else. His studio was just fifteen minutes away, in Norwalk.

It surprises me that I had forgotten about the photographer until now, twenty years later. A fourteen-year-old girl has been abducted; it's all over the national news. Photographs and videos reveal her insouciant smile, her gazelle body. My friends and I giggled and considered, though I do not know how seriously, the offer.

Joke

The young woman writer, until recently a student of the older man writer, sits on the banquette, kitty-corner to the older man writer, in the Rose Café on Fifth Avenue. It is *his* table. She has not been with a man who has *a table* since her grandfather, who had a table at a country club in Chicago. In that this is New York, and in that, at this time, according to the older man writer, movie-types and art-types such as Martin Scorsese and David Salle frequent this restaurant, it seems interesting that this man has a corner table reserved for him, nobody at it, and no reservation made, even at seven o'clock on a weekend.

The beautiful hostess brings them to the table. The young woman writer takes note of the beautiful clothes on the beautiful hostess, and she takes note of the way the older man writer speaks with intimate inflections to this woman. (She knows he does this with many women.)

They have dinner. And at dinner the older man writer suggests that the young woman writer not gobble the bread, as she is doing. They have not had sex, nor will they. In case that's what you were thinking.

After the bread, and after dinner (conversation was, as always, like a groomed lawn, soft, manicured, cool to the touch, soft again), the *dessert chef* shows up. She is also a beautiful woman. She flips the chair around and straddles it à la James Dean. She's got sinewy arms and strong features and her hair is in a ponytail. She's brought these desserts which look like abstract art sculptures. One for the older man writer, and one for the young woman writer. She says hi, kindly, to the young woman writer, and then talks to the older man writer.

"So, have I told you the one about the lawyer, the priest, and the Jew?"

Apparently she tells jokes in addition to making desserts. The older man writer makes that cute smile he makes sometimes and looks over his glasses at the dessert chef and begs her to go on. The young woman writer is also eager to hear the joke. She does not know how to tell jokes. She picks up her small fork and trails it around the raspberry sauce and up into the chocolate torte.

"Okay, so there was a lawyer, a priest, and a Jew. It was right after the winter holidays, and they were all taking a much-needed vacation. They were taking a cruise. In the Virgin Islands. Lovely. Beaches, naked women, the whole thing. Unfortunately, however, while they were sailing between islands, their cruise ship was torpedoed, yeah, unfortunately," here she shrugs, "and everyone died except, you guessed it, the lawyer, the priest, and the Jew. These three men swam to a deserted island. They lived there, eating coconuts and sardines, for a week. No other ships in sight. No airplanes. They were beginning to think they were forgotten, and they began to despair."

The young woman writer is listening. She's tasted the dessert, and it is yummy. The older man writer is eating his with gusto. He's not trailing his fork around.

"Just then a shark appeared. He said, 'I'll take you to the mainland. Just hop on my back.' Well, all three men were suspicious of the shark—but they were also desperate. The priest said, 'Okay, take me,' and he jumped on the back of the shark."

The young woman writer has never heard a woman tell this kind of joke before. Jokes such as this one are part of the male domain. They are related to bar stools, tartan shirts, fat bellies, baseball hats, drinks, and cigars—not to twenty-one-year-old women with fantastic arms and professional dessert-making jobs in New York City restaurants. In fact, the young woman writer had not even realized there would *be* a separate dessert chef. This is a new world, a world about which perhaps she will write, and of which perhaps she is, albeit in a tangential way, part?

"The shark started swimming away from the island with the priest on his back. But before he'd even gotten a hundred yards out, the shark flipped around and chomped the priest in half, then ate him all up. Okay. So the Jew and the lawyer are pretty sad about that. But they go about their business, eating sardines, drinking coconut milk, for another week. The shark shows up again and says, 'Hey, priests. What are you gonna do? But you two guys, upstanding sorts, I'd never eat you.' The Jew and the lawyer look at each other. They're pretty damn hungry at this point. The Jew is thinking about his kids back home. He's thinking he'd rather risk getting killed than stay on this godforsaken island. 'Okay, shark, take me to the mainland,' he says, and off he goes. But before he's even gotten a hundred yards, the shark flips around and chomps him in half and eats him all up."

The older man writer is giving all his attention to the beautiful dessert chef. The young woman writer has noticed that the beautiful dessert chef has a tattoo on her arm.

"The lawyer is watching from the shore. He can't believe it. He cries for the Jew, for the priest, but he is also crying for himself. How will he get off the island? He cracks open a coconut."

The older man writer has told the young woman writer, at times, that her writing is good. Quite good—exquisite. The older man writer has led the young woman writer to believe that her writing is, at times, as good, as lovely, as exquisite, as this dessert, this chocolate torte thing with funny cookies in it and raspberry sauce and bits of pistachio nut. It's not just chocolate cake, no. Not like that.

The older man himself, he writes brilliant, uncompromising books and has helped the young woman find herself as a writer. But as a person, with him, she is semi-lost.

"Now, another week passes, another two weeks. The shark is obviously keeping track of things. He's in the water, swimming back and forth. Then he comes up to shore and he says, 'Hey, lawyer, come on, I'll give you a ride.' Now, from experience, the lawyer knows that this shark is a liar and a killer. His two best friends, the priest and the Jew, have been eaten. But on the other hand, he's been on a deserted island for a month now and he's damn tired of it and besides, if he doesn't get his Lexus out of the hotel parking lot, it's going to get impounded. He knows it's almost useless, but what the hell, maybe he can fight the shark if he has to. Just get halfway to the mainland and swim. So he says, 'Okay, shark. I'm on.'"

The beautiful young hostess has come up and put her lovely arm around the beautiful dessert chef, and the beautiful dessert chef has raised her strong, dessert-making hand to the lovely skin of the hostess, and has settled it there.

"So the lawyer hops on the shark and the shark starts swimming obediently toward the mainland. Fifty yards. A hundred yards. A mile. Five miles. The lawyer is so amazed he isn't saying anything. He's just holding on to the shark's fins. Then there it is—the mainland! He sees it! The shark swims him all the way up to the private beach outside of this nice resort. He lets him off."

Now it's just the three of them again, a young woman writer, an older man writer, and a beautiful dessert chef. Beyond them, the din of the restaurant, many expensive dinners and glasses of wine being lost, consumed. The young woman writer has realized there is nothing as sexy as being a beautiful dessert chef telling a joke.

"The lawyer gets off and says, 'Thanks, shark. But listen, I don't understand. You ate the priest. You ate the Jew. Why'd you let me go?'"

"'Well,' said the shark, swimming away, 'I never eat my own kind.'"

A cigar, a tattoo, a turned chair. The dessert chef winks at the young woman writer and leaves her with the older man, and the young woman writer looks at the older man, filled as he is with sweet confection, and she wonders, mostly, about plot structure.

Wallet

We were in a city that saw little sunlight. All the buildings were gray, but there were also furtive things about it, furtive decorations: twisted angels, heroes, birds in flight. And there were the legendary finials and bulbs on top of the buildings. Downriver, heroes stood on the bridge in the dying, purple-strewn night. The swans pilfered the silence, and the horizon line, punctuated by the round and the straight, the golden and the violet, seemed mysterious and still tangible as nothing else ever had.

Underneath it all, people waited for buses and none of them were pretty and all of them wore double sweaters and carried fat, relentlessly used-up shopping bags. The young looked old and even the language was peculiar, zigzags and traffic jams.

My friend is a dominatrix. I had never seen her in character, but that night in the basement restaurant, eating something forgettable, drinking bad red wine, I saw her as they saw her.

The men at the other table were eager to make our acquaintance. Probably mainly hers, although I'd done my best to dress up. How to describe her beauty? She's tall and formidable. Imagine her as a Russian countess, black ermine muff or hooded fur coat and dark secrets and white snow and blood and wine (though usually she dresses in a T-shirt and jeans). That night she wore high black boots and a long leather coat. The men—middle-aged and gray-haired, not impressive or unique—asked where we were from, what we were doing, did we want to join them at their table? My instinct was no. She said yes. Like I said, I had never seen her in her professional role before. And she wasn't doing anything overt or physical that night, but her dominance was evident. She was aware of their expectations, their assumptions, and she was playing with them. Teasing them like a bored lion. (But if the rabbit *wants* to play, *wants* to die, who's in charge then?) I had been left in the dust.

We went to a bar for a drink and it seems to me now, though it's just a feeling, one of us was sitting on one of their laps. They were, naturally, paying. As we sat in our small huddle, the dark loud bar with a round table but only three available chairs, whiskeys in front of us, a sense on my part that I didn't know how long this would go on, how far it would go, a lack of ability to get my friend to the bathroom for a tête-à-tête, any kind of woman-to-woman reconnaissance, the men opened their wallets and showed us pictures of their children. You know the shot: a five-year-old, a two-year-old, crooked smiles and tight ponytails. It was a confession, a rite, and it came as no surprise to us, would-be-paramours, sad Americans, confused in love. From a distance, it's so clear. The two traveling salesmen. The potential one-night-stand, a little "good fun." A need, in any case, to put on the table the beauty in their lives, as well as the money for our drinks.

Boat

It was sinking. We had tried for years and it was still sinking. We had made light of our problems, we had even joked about them, and it was sinking. We had rented a new apartment together, one with beautiful light and clean wooden floors and we had a new puppy that cost three hundred dollars and it was still sinking. We were right for each other, we had even consecrated it through grief and laughter, and we had a decent amount of good times, and we thought we looked good together, which is something—some kind of balm—and it was sinking.

My friend laughed as the water spilled in, and then the three of us in the boat swam to shore. Luckily it was summer and the Merrimack is a fairly clean river. The he of the we did not laugh. Afterward, I stood on the pier, wet but not drowned. It was possible this would make a good story.

Pillbox

Originally given to Gloria by her mother, it was just a small gift accompanying something larger. That larger thing is lost; that larger thing could have been a sweater, an ocean liner, or a promise. For more years than anyone remembers, Gloria kept the pillbox on her vanity, near her hand mirror. These were the days of long, cream-colored Oldsmobiles—cars designed as living rooms—and glass-bellied lamps with womanly curves. The rose water and the Chanel No. 5 mingled with the faint smell of yesterday's gin martinis, and the wet smell of this evening's in particular.

The pillbox did not hold the actual pills she took, one after the other, three at a time washed down with that same gin, her stockings off but her blue chintz A-line dress still on, her pearls on, her Moroccan bracelet on, her earrings on. The pillbox, with its porcelain top and gold braid edge, with its haughty bouquet of never-ending odorless flowers, simply bore witness, vessel essence in tact, emptiness untampered with, sightless eyes open.

Unremembered Thing

It's close to where the sock goes. In the night, right before sleep, or even in the middle of the night, a dream, a revelation, the thought comes to you. It's complete. It's beautiful. It's perfect. In fact, it's so perfect that you're sure you will remember it tomorrow, for it's the nexus of all things, it's the key to your project. It's like a mandala or an icon. And the wonderful thing is that it's living, it's breathing. It will flow through your project and make things right, tie up the loose ends. Essentially, it's the finishing touch. It's the fucking *door* to the fucking *house*.

And you are pretty damn sure you would never forget something as important and perfect as this. It just makes too much sense. But still, just to make sure, you repeat the key word to yourself a few times before you drift back to sleep. "_____," "_____," "_____." You consider writing it down, but you don't think the pen is any longer in the drawer, and even if it is, you have no paper here . . . so you go back to sleep.

Purse

She wants him to care about it. She wants him to notice the lines of it, the stitching. He is vacillating between looking at her eyes, which are crackling with anger, and what is in her hand: a purse from the vendor.

He'd only called her again because he was lonely and wanted company, not because he in particular needed *her* company. Even a mall can be the site of spiritual compromises of the most complex and life-altering kind.

Still, he knows her: knows her body, knows her moods. He knows a little about how she dresses. He tries to employ some of this knowledge in this situation: does he like this black, squareish purse more than the more narrow, floppier black purse, or does he like the small red purse?

Good fucking God, he doesn't care.

"I don't know, like I said. But this one is, you know, it's cool. It's . . . pretty," he says.

"Yeah, but, do you think it's, like, too clunky for just walking around?"

"No." Shrug.

"I don't know. It seems too much like my old one, you know? Maybe it's time for a change."

"Yeah, maybe. That sounds good."

"Although, on the other hand, I *like* my old one."

"So why not keep your old one?"

Now she shrugs. "I don't know. I'm kind of bored with it."

"Oh, okay."

"So do you like this one? As much as the one I have now?"

"Sure. Yeah."

"What do you mean, 'Sure'?"

"What do you mean what do I mean?"

"Well, you sound doubtful."

Jesus. "Look, I think it's nice. I mean it."

The young woman considers this purse for another thirty seconds, and then lets it fall down to the crook of her arm, and she regards the other purse—the small red one.

"This one is so cute, though."

"Yeah, it is," he says. Looking around.

"This one would go nice with my red pants, too."

"Yeah, you'd be all red," he says. It sounds more sarcastic than he means it to.

"That was a fucked-up thing to say."

"What the—" he starts, and then says, "Look, I only meant it would go with your red pants, like you said."

"Yeah, it would, but the way you said it sounded like, I don't know—like you were making fun of me or something." She looks at the purse vendor, an Asian man sitting on a stool reading a magazine, and then at another shopper, a middle-aged woman with one hand on a stroller.

"Look, Jules, as far as I'm concerned, they're all nice purses. You know? Like they are all such nice purses that *who the fuck cares* which one you take anyway?"

The young woman starts putting all three purses, one after the other, kind of roughly, back on the pegs.

"What are you doing? C'mon, aren't you getting one?"

"No, I'm *not* getting one."

"Why not? Get the red one. I like the red one."

"I don't even give a shit what you like. You're so clueless when it comes to these things." She is pretty much hissing the words and he knows this is going to fuck up at least a good part of the afternoon, in fact, the afternoon already feels long gone. He'd had hopes, plans.

"Jules, Julie. I'm sorry. I'm so sorry." He holds onto her arm as she starts walking toward the Gap.

Julie puts her head down. She doesn't speak.

"Jules, honey babe? C'mon, I'm sorry. It's just that to me—to me—I like care about you but I don't care as much about the purses, all right? I trust your judgment about what purse is the right one, okay?"

"I just, I just want to, you know, get taken seriously when I ask you a question. And, and, I want to look good for you."

"You always look good to me, Jules, no matter what purse you've got on your arm. You'd look better if the purse had a couple grand in it, but other than that—"

He smiles at her and leans his head in, touches her chin with his cupped hand. She's grinning now, at the mall floor. Then she looks up at him.

Glass

There was once a glass, and in the glass was a tulip. I wrote a poem about this. The tulip had been given to me by the man I was sleeping with in clandestine fashion. Well, not *sleeping*, exactly, just toppling each other on hillsides, in hallways. The orange tulip. The thing about it is this: it fucking grew even after it was cut.

Rabbits

The first time the rabbits died it was spring, and she hardly knew what to think about the Wyoming testimony—the Godlike wind in the cottonwoods, the way the lightning cracked your skull wide open and made you see things in X-ray. She crept. She followed her friend, who acted as guide.

They were coming back from Walmart or somewhere, back to the friend's trailer on company land. The boss man was filthy rich and old and loved his guns. They opened up the gate and the friend showed off her little garden, and then they walked up to the front porch.

Four dead baby rabbits lay in a line on the top step. In the garbage can they found three others.

The garbage can was actually a "burn barrel"—here's where you burned trash yourself about once a week, spilled a little kerosene in there and lit a match. It stunk, yes, but it did the job and you didn't need to wait for any damn government truck.

He must have done this, the friend said. He hates rabbits.

The newcomer took pictures of the rabbits as evidence of something, but when she sent the photographs back to New York, the package got lost in the mail.

Two years later the newcomer lived in Wyoming herself, up a hill, in another house on company land, a geodesic dome. She drove the beat-up old station wagon that her friend had sold her. She drove it up the dirt road, up the dark hill to her house after a night at the bar.

At that time of year you had to drive slowly, because the rabbits had recently given birth, and there were swarms—millions, zillions—of darting rabbits on the dirt road. On either side of the road was a field with warrens and streams and all kinds of rabbit habitat. They came out at night.

It was as if the baby rabbits didn't yet know the danger of cars, or perhaps they were just so multitudinous that they hopped everywhere, road or no road. Anyway, you had to drive slowly not to hit them.

And she did drive slowly.

The rabbits came out every night, the baby rabbits, and they were like small gray streaks on the road, you could hardly see them before they were there, in front of you, streaking across the dirt, zigzagging around, frantic, stupid. She leaned forward, holding onto the steering wheel. She honked.

But to really ensure their well-being, you'd just have to turn the car off and walk. Night after night, on her way home from the bar, she drove on. There would be bumps. She began to drive a little faster over the hill. Like she belonged here. Like the rabbits would disappear, as the dead ones on the porch did, even the photos of them.

There were so many rabbits, after all. In a few months she herself would be gone.

Big Truck

Once you've been with a guy who has a big truck, there's no going back. It's depressing but true, it's like falling off a cliff. May as well just slit your wrists, dig a hole, write the obituary. Once you've felt that strong rumble underneath—I mean a *really* strong rumble. I mean the engine turning over and doing those other things engines do. Idling, feeling power. You're sitting at a red light, and there it is, all that power underneath you, all around you, jiggling your bangles, making it hard to light a cigarette, making you have to go to the bathroom, making the poetic stare hard to maintain as you listen for the illustrative comment—once you've been there, I'd say it's like being present when a star is created, up way up where these things happen, these mysteries, these strong beautiful mysteries of destruction and creation. There you are sitting on top of the fucking star. Everything is there, everyone is there, you see it all. Everything is pure blackness. Everything is pure blissful obliterating light. And it's all right where it should be—sound—sight—and you're shouting your *ears* off, you're shouting uncontrollably words you never knew and then it's all gone again, a pinpoint of silence and a dawn/gray-sheet kind of thing, a light green kind of thing, and you have no thoughts and you're not shouting anymore. You are so refined, your essence is so stunned and thin, that the physical you sitting on the hot plastic seat sweating and human no longer shakes with power. You're beyond the shaking, you're pure with it now. And then there's the turn signal, the green arrow. Some of the sad little pathetic cars gun their sad little mosquito engines, little secretaries and little attorneys and little clerks and little tiny business owners, and little unemployed people, they all try to gun it in their pathetic little cars, twenty, thirty feet down from you, it's like killing flies or flicking crumbs, but for them it's everything, you can hear them pushing their little feet down to the floor of their automatic used hatchbacks, and they putt-putt out and try to beat the light. Not your man, though, and his fine truck. A truck as big as a building, but more outrageous, capable and outrageous as the ocean, imagine the ocean, and then imagine the transmutation of glass and steel and imagine the energy underneath like a force beyond all human comprehension, a force that underscores all we do, is who we are, is who we are if we are anything, if we understand, understand where it all comes from, damn, divine, damn, and so this truck doesn't fucking have to try to beat any goddamned light; this truck just moves. It just moves like a continent. And then you're on the other side of the road and you see East like a vision and you've got the runway ahead of you and you fucking *go*, I mean you fucking *go*—oh, Delta, American, United—those sops need to share the power. You don't need to share anything.

Have I mentioned stopping at the convenience store? Because this is where things get really crazy. I mean this is another place where things heat up for you. So you're there, right, and you can see the roof of the 7-11, and somewhere down there are the Supplies—some cherry 7-Up, and some cigarettes, and some Pringles perhaps. And you're in a truck like the Space Needle in Seattle or like the Empire State

Building or like the Great Wall of China, or maybe just like goddamn planet Earth compared to the rest of the half-assed, jerry-rigged, keep-us-in-orbit planets, and you've got to open the door. And he's maybe given you a twenty, a whole twenty, and so you try to open the door but it doesn't open, man it's a heavy door, this handle, it's hard to get open, and he leans over and he kind of flips it and shoves, and there it is—freedom, the sky, a short flight to the 7-11, and you're thinking, parachute? And he lets you in on something, a little secret: *I like women who do it their own way. I like women with their own strength and style.* And so he's sitting there, his arms half leaning on the steering wheel, a massive chrome wheel, like a windmill with a rim, and he's waiting for you to do your own thing, trot into the convenience store—with strength, with style. And so you take off—you fucking take off—and you're flying down and you can do it! And before you know it, you're back! And you've got the soda, you've got the snack food! And you're now, blessedly, back at home, back in the truck, and it's so damn exhilarating, it's like nothing else, and now you can go home and make love like equals, briefly like equals . . . but all the while you're not thinking of him, you aren't, you can't, you can't or it all stops, the gears get jammed up, the light is lost again, the road is a challenge. No, you need to return to the truck. The lavish, gleaming truck. The lavish, gleaming truck with the fat wheels the size of unique countries, and the life force involved some-where, internally, in height, in sound, in the placement of the constellations in the brute night sky. Give me the truck or give me nothing. Stay away from the little cars; go gently toward steel and glass and enjoy with me the dream of a free world, a nation undivided by squirrels and weakness.

Gun

He was from Alabama. I don't know if that means anything
to you, or maybe he was from Tennessee, because there was
the Elvis thing, though that may have been an interstate
love, no boundaries. Alabama. Sweet Home Alabama, De-
liverance—no, that was Georgia. Look, I don't know much
about Alabama, but I'm a sucker for any kind of accent,
even a strange tin-can twang like his. He, the man in a
black leather coat, long like a rock star or Count Dracula.
He also had long hair and you'd think, oh, okay, Southern Rock, but no, he was into some kind of Elvis-meets-
technology shit and that's what he did on his keyboard but
he always used headphones so none of us really knew, we
all kept guessing, giving him the benefit of the doubt. It
was entertaining, in a cocktail party way, that this Southern Rock/redneck guy was also an Artist. A fancy pants
Musician. It was like his long hair was some kind of "long
hair" and his affinity for Elvis was some kind of "affinity
for Elvis" and his Dracula coat was a "Dracula coat" and
then also that the gun was a "gun" but perhaps that's where
the irony leaves off, with the iron so to speak: all you've
got left is why. Why did he show me the gun? Why did he
have the gun with him at the artists' colony, this enclave
of gracious living, this ivory tower? The gun was wrapped
in a piece of fabric. He held it between us for a moment,
and then he uncovered it. There it was, black and modern.
Pig-modern, square modern, like you'd see in the gangster
movies today, or on the cop shows. Not an old "gun"—the

romantic kind, that also killed people, but had some kind
of whatever attached. This was a new-death gun, state-of-
the-art automatic weapon. All the artists around me were
concerned about whether the coffee in the carafe was half-
decaf, half-caf, or if the cookies on the plate were yesterday's batch or this morning's. Meanwhile Alabama, Alabama—was he wooing me? Was this love?

Dishes the Cat Used, Now Stored in the Laundry Room

The small white house sits on the edge of the park overlooking a river. It features a glassed-in porch and a history. She died, the old nurse, and her family has hired an auction company to dispense with her belongings. A teenager trudges out of the house with boxes. Furniture is on the lawn.

I didn't know this woman, and neither did my husband, though this is his hometown. We have come here on vacation. A week ago, we put our cat to sleep. He was eighteen and sick, about to really hit the skids, and we hastened the process. The vet gave him a first shot to relax him. As it took effect, his face changed. He looked like a kitten.

Here is a box of sewing things. Here is a box of linens. Here is a hamper with laundry still in it, and here is her Christmas tree stand. Here is a mirror I could send back to Tucson and put in my bathroom: a bargain. A bag of buttons, a checked parasol, a 1950s luggage set, a stack of books, a carton of loose photographs, a jewelry box, a shoe horn, a knick-knack shelf, crystal wineglasses, a '79 Buick with twelve thousand miles on it, an antique chair one of the rifling neighbors says "was her pride and joy, was her favorite."

After the second shot, the vet checked for a heartbeat and found none. He retreated to other, shallower parts of the clinic, leaving us alone. The cat lay on the steel table, a swell of gray stomach. Was he really dead? His body was still warm. He was the cat who lay on the lawn, gleaning coolness in the evening. In recent days he'd begun to meow all the time, a last hard song.

The auctioneer's voice is impressive, almost kind. Men stand on the raised platform and hold up dolls, pillowcases. People buy boxes for two dollar two dollar two dollar two dollar one dollar one dollar one dollar. Look at this: the way she folded that blanket the woman is lifting out of a basket dubiously, as if it may or may not be valuable to someone.

Where is she now, the nameless nurse? Did she look down on the auction, and was she appalled? Did it come to nothing, then: the photographs, the cards kept for decades, the lamp that never quite worked, the baby booties—stuffed into black bags, scattered across town—or did she make a clean break, is she free and jumpy and far away, humming or purring in some impossible final dawn?

Talk

Don't get too bored. I just want to talk. The thing is, I re-member talking to those guys into the wee hours. Talk, talk, talk. I wore them out with my talking. It's obvious when I think about it what they wanted from me. It wasn't a question of love, or friendship. They'd try to talk me into it, and I'd try to talk us out of it. Talk, talk, talk. Hours passed, hard-ons drooped. I waited them out like a hunter, waiting for the ducks at daybreak. Then I'd get up, adjust my pink bra, and go home, quiet.

Pain

The pain occurs to me, and then I put words to the pain, and before long I am in a cardboard box hurtling through time. The appointment is at 4:45 on Thursday afternoon; be there at 4:30 if you don't mind.

The first tip-off is the whispery shuffling of the quiet women in teal shirts. There are many of them, eight or twelve, and their hair is all fluffed and brown with attractive blond streaks, and they range from twenty to forty-five years old. Each has a nameplate featuring the place she was born, like those worn by college-age waitresses in tourist zones. Idaho hands me a Naugahyde folder with some forms and a pen, pre-opened. I am eyeing the refrigerator full of complementary beverages—*Have one!*

The medical information form concludes with a series of faces, smiling to grimacing, and I'm meant to check which expression matches my current emotional state. I can't choose just one; I add arrows to indicate the complexity of it all. Before long a whispery woman with submissive shoulders creeps up and asks if I would like to go back to the room now. I follow her past a few posted pledges of compassion and kindness and then the regular diplomas. A whole new geography of women in teal shirts lives back here, and as I slip into the examination room they smile meekly in my direction and nod. I have my ears perked for screams or moans but hear nothing. Reluctantly I sit down. Would I like to listen to some jokes on tape, or perhaps Mozart? No thanks. Am I at all chilly, does she need to turn the AC down? Would I like to put my purse over here, where I can see it? Would I like a magazine or a book? They have the newest Danielle Steel.

Preliminary procedures begin and they are mild: the initial work includes putting cardboard squares and plastic spoons in my mouth and rolling them around. The doctor will be here soon, whispers a brown-haired girl from Oklahoma. Her breath smells like roses and mint gum. Her skin is hairless and uniform in color, and her little white hands are dewy and trembling. Would I like a short foot massage while I'm waiting? Well, all right. She says, no, let me, and pulls off my shoes, one after the other, and then she takes the first foot in one hand and rolls off my sock, too, and then it's the other foot's turn. She encircles my foot with warmth, and then she notices the embarrassed cold look of its mate, reaches over for the sweater hanging on a chair and wraps the waiting foot in that. The doctor comes in. He's white-haired and stolid and solid, too. He pulls out a stool. Now, he says, tell me everything. Wait a minute—he stands back up and dims the lights so that the equipment gleams like stars lit by a golden moon. Where to begin? Is it all right if I tell you a little bit about my parents first? By all means, he says. Take your time.

While I'm talking, the food cart arrives. Actually, there are two—the savory and the sweet selections, a teal-shirted whispery submissive woman smiling over each one. I wave away savory and ask sweet to come forward. Always the difficulty: which to choose, whether to go chocolate or lemon. Or apple, in certain circumstances. Pineapple? I choose the éclair this time, and Oklahoma lets go of the second foot, wraps them both in the cashmere, and lifts her shoulders and giggles conspiratorially when, after I've taken a big bite, a glop of filling falls onto my hand. She licks it off with her slightly rough tongue.

The doctor says, let's take a break and enjoy life while you're eating. And I say, why don't you eat, too? Ah, he says, patting his belly three times. Mustn't. But don't let that stop your enjoyment. Here, I'll just take a brief toke from this hookah. The equipment, which I'd imagined, of course, as designed to simultaneously repair and heal and cause pain, also appears to have a pipe mechanism. Between tokes, the doctor gazes into my eyes and murmurs guesses about my age. Surely you're what, twenty, twenty-one? I let my eyes go all catlike and murmur back at him.

After snacks and after I've finished my life story, the doctor says, well, we best get back to business, hmm? And he says, now, you know this won't hurt a bit, right? The friendly helper is showering my feet with ginger-scented talcum powder, and blowing between the toes to make the shimmering white dust uniform. I hope not, I say. Doctor keeps gazing into my eyes. May I? He brings his hands to my hair, and as he plunges his fingers in, as I feel the enclosure of his arms, I get the faintest whiff of his cologne, or his underarm scent, a kind of husky safe smell, no stains at all on the blue cotton.

He continues to draw his fingers through my hair and then he says, what were we thinking? Melissa, sweetheart, would you mind hooking up the gas? This poor young lady may be suffering. I'm smiling back into his glasses. I see my own reflection multiplied a hundred times. I choose the "pink" gas, and Melissa—for that is the lovely girl's name—positions the contraption over my nose. She places the dial in my hand and I am free to increase or decrease the strength of the drug at whim. I breathe in.

The doctor begins the procedure. He shows me the scalpel's edge. It is gleaming silver, the shiniest thing. We've changed the lighting back—not to awfully, consistently bright, but to a kind of mood lighting that involves targeted radiant spheres of illumination. Holding the scalpel in front of my face, he slowly turns it so I can appreciate it from many angles. I long to touch the edge—it almost sharpens into nothing! The edge seems to go on into infinitesimal sharp sharpness, a half-inch or even an inch past the visible, into the imagined.

One of the original problems with the pain was that it moved around; the root location had yet to be determined. Melissa exposes one part of my body at a time. They begin with my neck, first breathing softly near it, murmuring to each other. They have a sweet, ongoing relationship—intimate but inclusive. I am now part of the triad, the trio, the triage. I alternate between closing my eyes, experiencing soft slow fireworks behind my eyelids, and opening them again, localizing and then relocalizing sensation. Melissa has covered my neck now with a gossamer scarf, and she has lifted my T-shirt to expose my stomach. A narrative has formed in my head, which I suspect has been revealed by the truth of the pink gas, and I settle back into it, lay into it, like a hammock. I savor and repeat, and I feel the pressure of the chill blade, and then the pulsing, exorbitant release that comes from the exposure of my inner, private self, to the air of the room. They move on to the other side of my rib cage. They move to my breast. My underarm. The doctor is telling me the quiet secrets of his own life as he

works, and Melissa, who knows what I need, who is pre-
scient, perhaps psychic, keeps my skin the right tempera-
ture, and now and then strokes, as if unconsciously, the top
of my hand. It is her hand, my hand, and the gas meter, as
one. I have begun to realize that the secrets of the doctor's
life have merged with my own, and that in that synergy or
parallelism, in that conversation, is a kind of grander realization—something necessary and frankly profound, albeit
quite simple, for the whole world, for peace on earth, and
for the unification of all natural species and even plants. A
little blip in time occurs and now they are both asking me if
I would but roll over, just to my side? Not certain how long
they've been asking me this—a second, ten? With Melissa's
help, I turn—a slight disruption, a forgetfulness regarding
the story's thread, but I crank up the dial on the pink and
soon I'm settled in again. The doctor is rubbing his palm
around my right buttock, as if searching for something,
for the right angle. He puts his head down, listens. For a
moment I feel the wisps of his white hair, the hair of a god,
on my skin; it is the tactile manifestation of light rays coming in. For this we'll need a bigger blade, he tells Melissa.
Of course, she says, and leaves off her attendance briefly
to reach for the silver box of tools on the nearby swiveling
shelf. She has trouble opening it, and places the discarded
small scalpel in her teeth as she opens and reveals the set
of implements: silver, sharp, brilliant. Ah, he says, once
again lovingly caressing the knife before using it. Allow-
ing me to see it first—as you show a child, for instance, the
thermometer before sticking it in.

I don't think I'm fully feeling what happens next, but
whatever it is seems to actually increase sensation in some

way, for a surge of emotion, a wave of language, explodes under my eyes, and it is fierce and pleasurable, even as it unsettles me. Afterward, I am breathless, grateful, and yet almost regretful that it's over, that the sound of things has once again quieted down. My fingers on the dial once more.

They turn me on my belly after that and work on my shoulder blades, one at a time, and then on my upper left thigh. When they are done, they return me to my back. The gossamer completely covers me now, a web of silken threads. The music in the room has also returned, a counter-narrative to the drug, and I am briefly suspicious that, like a second brake in a driver's ed car, there is some other dial, manned by someone else—Melissa? the doctor?—that can diminish the pink gas even as I turn it up toward maximum. The food-cart women are back; I see them out of the corner of my eye, but I do not want a savory now, on top of the sweet. Too much—not the right combination, not the right order to things. Melissa and the doctor are speaking to each other, laughing about something that happened at the office party last week, last season. I feel the knit of the stitches throughout my body, and they, anyway, are a tremendous relief, a relic of my existence. Melissa rolls my socks back onto my feet, kissing one then the other, before she pushes my shoes back on. The shoes are small weights, like anchors, dragging at me. The doctor is writing notes. His back is turned. Good, strong back! Good, strong man! But he is not the psychic one—when I think this, the yearning thought, he does not turn around. Melissa smiles down at me, Oklahoma, and she is clasping her hands together, returned to herself. But where is Oklahoma, really? I have never been there. I imagine wheat, sunshine, perhaps cows. But how does that compare to pain? Where did my pain go? Melissa, Melissa, where did my pain go? The gossamer is lifting. My feet are heavy now and you are leaving me, you are leaving!

Ambition

At first you have your feet in the sand and you are standing, see, but then the water seeps in and you're up to your waist, then armpits, then neck, then you are simply keeping your head above water, and so you float—jump—and up you go, chin high, feet liberated and wiggling, knees light and bicycling, arms useful now and dancing; you are always just a little higher than your failure.

Motherhood

In the distance, on the dream line of the road, they look not like birds so much as the twinkling reflection of sunlight on a lake, the way light hops from place to place. But as I drive closer I realize that it's a mother quail—the Gambel's Quail that have astonished me here, with their fat prettiness and their pompadours—and her dozen or so tiny chicks. They are attempting to cross the street, thirty-miles-an-hour speed limit but most people here in Tucson drive faster. I am hitting my brakes and wondering how to warn everyone, fumbling for the emergency blinkers. The baby birds are right in the middle of the road, and the mother is herding them south, then changing her mind and going back where she came from. The sparks of fluff and light follow along, one, then the other, then five—and then two head off on their own in the other direction. One of today's monster trucks, red with an eagle wings decal on the back window, hurtles past me and right over, right through. In the wake of his (why do I think of it as "his"? Nothing says it couldn't have been a woman in that truck) no-brake run, I see the aftermath. They've been hit. Damage is done. No longer a sprightly trail of life forms, but a mother, intact, a few of her babies left standing, and then some completely flattened, and then some half-wrecked but still moving after a fashion—perhaps there's some kind of momentum even after life is for all intents and purposes gone, or they are being blown by wind from the truck's passage, or perhaps it is determination to keep up in their flawed path behind their mother, or perhaps it is just terror.

Okay, so she has a birdbrain, the mother. So she's a bird. But it was in her to herd and shuffle around this family of a dozen wobbling chicks, to nip and squawk at them when they didn't follow, when they veered off from her path; it was in her to keep them with her, to feed them, to be their mother. What is she going to do now? How does the anxiety, the sadness, the discontent, the unfairness, manifest in her? For it does, it will, and whether it is intellect, emotion, instinct, doesn't matter, for it—motherhood—is physical at its core.

On my way back, when I passed that way again, there wasn't even a sign of the flattened babies. There was so little to them—half a cup of feathers, two toothpicks, and the life force—that they just blew away and were gone.

Loss Itself

The man was large, though not because he ate a lot of fast food, or not solely because of that. He was an artist, he'd taken in a great many things in his life, and he didn't have the time or inclination to fuck with diets. His thick, shaking hand held the paintbrush.

Sometimes there was no paintbrush. Some days the paintbrush itself became the airbrushed painting of a paintbrush in an airbrushed café. It became, as if, awful and depressing as all the crap in a dump of crap, all the deep dumpy crap that accumulates.

Still he held the paintbrush in his warm hand. His hand was a vivid reminder, the sense that vividness itself can wear mittens, that we labor against our inability to be precise, to call into being what we experience and see.

But he did labor to call into being. He did labor to see.

Kitchen

The table is sticky. "Butcher Block"—a new concept for the era. You need to oil it every couple of months to keep it fresh. There's a fine sediment, a film, that never comes off. If you keep your elbows on it too long you make a slow noise when you tear away.

The clock stares from above the door. It ticks; the refrigerator makes a warm hum. The mother fills the refrigerator and the daughter empties it, basically. The daughter enters the kitchen and, nine times out of ten, opens the refrigerator, looks in, maybe gets something, closes the door, and turns away. It's as if she's checking on incubating eggs. She doesn't have to be hungry.

Out the window in front of the kitchen sink you can see the garden and part of the yard. Sometimes you can see the dog rolling around in the grass, or one of the family cats walking a railroad tie that separates the strawberries from the herbs from the cucumbers, or sitting, head bent, waiting to pounce on something.

The kitchen is all orange. It's got brick orange floors and bright *bright* orange linoleum counters. Everyone in the family knows the map of the cabinets, knows where the raisins are, the teaspoons, the pudding, the matches.

Even when the daughter is relentlessly interested in everything else in the world, the smell of her mother's brown rice or her mother's broccoli or ratatouille or her mother's pesto fills her like no other food, no other smell. Right now there's something boiling, and the daughter is sitting at the table, elbows glued to the wood, and she is staring at the clock aimlessly and telling her mother about the guy she likes, Dan. The daughter is fifteen and the mother is thirty-seven. The mother loves love stories.

It's a lost, delicious feeling, knowing you have a lot of time. Besides the radical joy of her feelings about Dan, there is the additional joy of telling the story of Dan to another, to her mother, and thus to make it more real . . . to make it tick like the clock.

Now there is no trace of Dan.

The kitchen was orange, I'm telling you. And there were murmurs, strong and regular along with the clink of the metal bowl and the hush of the tap water and the *chop, chop, chop* of tomatoes for dinner.

Bratz Doll

The child got two Bratz dolls for her birthday from "someone she didn't like very much." And she didn't really like Bratz dolls either, and the entire birthday party's worth of little girls put the dolls through the wringer. They cut the first doll's hair to shoulder length, then they marked up her face with pens. Then they put her in the pool to drown her. At first, my daughter tells me, the doll's head bobbed above the surface. They went to work on the second. They cut her hair, too, all the way to the scalp. They pulled off her head and then "by mistake" someone cut her in half. By this time the other doll had drifted down to the pool's floor.

Boots

The friend had done you a favor. The friend had done a generous thing. No one had any money back then. The idea was maybe the friend could take the boots as payment. They were blue—turquoise, really. The friend tried on the boots in your bedroom. You and the friend were on the skids, man. You and the friend—something bitter to the taste, something poison. The friend sat down and pulled on the boots. They were boots you'd given yourself for your birthday one summer in New Mexico. Whatever, the friend could have them. Maybe it would help. She pulled on one boot then the other then got up and walked around a little, looking down.

"They fit?"

"They fit, maybe. Maybe they're a little tight."

"You can have them if you want."

The friend shrugged. Took them off. Neither of you mentioned them again, the turquoise boots, the transaction, the failed transaction, the thing the boots were payment for, the friendship, the failed friendship, the possibility of change.

Cigarette

It is a night like any other, except for the visitation. I put my head on the pillow, ready for bed. My eyes are focused on the night table, on the clock, the lamp, the books, the glass of water. My eyes see the little bit of busy fabric on the pillow. My eyes see the gentle stripes of the quilt.

I smell it.

Wait.

Just a tiny—just a fragment, a trace, a little ghost trace. It's on my pillow. But no one smokes here. I haven't smoked for years. No one has visited us. It must be from long ago—or just the night before—when my lover and I smoked together, after we made love on these sheets, this pillow, from when we were smoking and laughing and drinking seltzer with lemon and eating chocolate—yes, we smoked a cigarette then, after the red; we lit it tenderly for one another, a shared moment of repose, contentment, letting our hearts slow down, become quiet; sweat drying off, blood pumping slower and the quilt pulled up.

But then I don't smell it anymore. Perhaps I can re-animate this—just this one moment. I sit back up. I lie back down. I sniff at the fabric eagerly—faith, memory, desire— and smell nothing at all.

Stone

The man put the small stone on the table in the apartment he was using that month between trips: he was a race-car driver and always had a place to go, a place of driving quite fast and circularly. The girl stared at the stone, her eyes big as—

Her parents were Southern Christians and—

But the small stone of course had a life of its own, so to speak, before the girl or the man came along to imbue it with mistaken identities. The stone was resolute in its shape, size, density. It was perfectly pleased to be alone, or to be among other stones. It had been in a river. It had been part of a gravel path. It had been pitched into a field by a child.

The stone did not need stories, did not need strife. The stone was quiet and peaceful and had one small nick in it, as if it could, in fact, also erode.

Aurelie Sheehan

Old Boyfriend

Once I said, when we weren't even breaking up for the first time, that if you married someone else, if I imagined her with you—in a house, in the kitchen, in the bedroom, with children—it would be as if she were an interloper in our dream. How odd it was to imagine. It was a kind of self-ishness, then, or understanding, that made me hold on. You understood the feeling, I think, and I also think you would understand now as I—on the brink of getting married—seek you, to say goodbye, to say again how much I loved you, how wrong I was in the mistakes I made. This is a shell within a shell at the bottom of the ocean. I covered things up, with the idea that no one would ever get hurt. Little kindness.

Kleenex Box

The dominatrix has a Kleenex box on her table when she makes the call. She is a dominatrix, as I said, but she is more and other than that. She is, true story, a human being. She makes the call: I'm back, she says, to the man who answers.

What is a man? A man I know said he wasn't much of a man. He didn't have that much testosterone, he said. This man is a fine specimen of manhood, physically speaking, robust, etc., and, while his wife works during the day, he cares for their children.

I was driving home the other day and I saw this bumper sticker: *Because I have a penis, that's why.* In my mod new car, thirty-eight years old, not made-up, I squinted at the bumper sticker, trying to understand irony in it. It was on the window of a truck. The guy driving had a shaved head. As I drove past, I saw he had an urgent, entirely unironic look. The truck also had one of those stickers with a kid pissing on something: in this case, a Chevy logo.

Speaking of my new car, it's really my husband's and my new car, but my husband always refers to it as my new car, and he has invited me to, or he insists that I drive it on a regular basis, while he drives the old car.

When my parents got a new car, my mother drove it. My parents got divorced later. With my husband, though, it's different—I like to think this, in any case.

But maybe that's beside the point. The dominatrix is going back in business today, even though her allergies are acting up, because she needs money to pay the mortgage and support her two daughters. The fathers are not here. One is an ex-marine. It always seemed like a good match, in terms of fierceness, for an ex-marine and a dominatrix to get together. I don't know anything about the other guy.

The dominatrix, I mean the human being with a leather outfit in her closet, the mother of two daughters, hangs up the phone after making the appointment and leans over to the table and plucks a tissue from the box.

What is a man? What does it mean to piss on someone?

Devotion

In the pew in front of me sat two teenage sisters, come along with their short father and tall mother. The parents were holding hands and staring toward the altar.

Soon after the service began, the older sister leaned forward and put her head down. The younger one, with longer hair, trailed her fingers across her sister's back, lightly scratching her T-shirt. She ran her fingers up over the ribs, then down again, circling around the small of her sister's back, and then up the other side, and then plunging her hand to the nape of the neck, under her sister's hair. When she was done, she leaned forward.

The older sister pushed the younger one's blond hair out of the way, some to one side, some to the other. Then she danced her fingers up and down her sister's back. This girl had a more desultory technique, casual and confident. Her wrist bent back, then swung forward. She paused, the priest implored, she resumed. Her fingertips trailed over her sister's ribs, up and down her spine. She too swooped up to the neck and let her fingers rest there.

The sisters never spoke. They took second, then third turns.

AURELIE SHEEHAN

Mushroom Paté

There was a time when no one really knew what paté was. It seemed paté was like chip dip, only you didn't call it chip dip, and it also seemed that paté was like mashed liverwurst, or perhaps the gross bottom of the pan where the Thanksgiving turkey had been prior to the slashing.

At the time, too, a fashion cropped up for vegetarianism. I know. I myself tinkered with this diet. In any case, the vegetarian chef, twenty-four—ancient to me then, now bizarrely young—the reggae-listening, Japanese-watercolor-painting, reefer-smoking, trust-fund-collecting chef for whom I worked cutting vegetables and making salads at a restaurant, itself called The Mushroom, which catered to the new vegetarianism, in a high-class town called Westport, Connecticut, taught me how to make mushroom paté one afternoon.

Oh, I was excited. It would be relevant to learn how to mash mushrooms and cook them in a new way with basil and red wine and other mashed things. Certainly it was only the beginning of my adventures, my education, my sophisticated life at sixteen. He told me, for instance, *not* to use the bunched-up paper towel to hold the butter hunk as I buttered the pan. He told me instead to use my fingers. For it was a sensual thing.

I set the paper towel aside. I needed to get back home by six in order to eat with my family. Still together at the time. I stuck my never-had-an-orgasm-with-a-man, never-really-said-to-anyone-but-my-best-friend-how-I-real-

ly-felt-about-anything, totally-invisible-at-school, totally
confused fingers into the butter and bore down. The oily
creamy white was a small, flattering indiscretion, better,
in any case, than the paté. I never really got it off my hand.

AURELIE SHEEHAN

Quote

I am dubious about it; I hope it's true.

The mythology tells us the opposite; the mythology is all about the individual artist and about his or her—mostly his—sacrifice. Sex is all right, though. In fact, you're expected to have a passionate fling or twenty, so long as they end badly. But marriage? Likely to be (a) sterile or (b) destructive or (c) both. There are certain examples otherwise, but we view them suspiciously. One woman we can think of has a high-pitched, totally lunatic reading voice; her husband killed himself after all.

Yet aren't all lives lives of art, really? Whether it's taking DJ lessons or refurbishing antique cars or climbing up the slide with your three-year-old, hacking away at invisible vines with a plastic sword?

On the other hand, these guys, the ones on PBS—surely they were thinking only about art with a big A.

Matisse said it, and then my husband turned to me and said it, and then he said it again. On the television, there are stills of the old man in his beret feeding a cat some croissant or some brie, and in the background are the canvases, an embodiment. "Was he married?" I ask. We don't know; we came to the special late. But we do agree with what he said. We know and we hope and when we aren't hoping we're sure and when we're not sure we hope.

Tail

The door shuts, but there's still a little air, a little light coming from that corner. An accident, a mistake, a mischance: the cat had made a run for it. Two inches of shorn fur, with skin, and no cat proper to be seen until two hours later, when he slinks across the living room, tail bones bare.

Off to the vet, amputation of the bare bones, and back home for the evening.

The cat is wide-eyed from anesthesia, his gaze blurred and bright. He sits in the doorway where it happened. As if to remember, to make sense of this landmark. What *did* happen? Is this the sign of terrible new luck? Cosmic wrongdoing? From our perspective, the cat doesn't seem too upset about his shaved, shorter tail. And yet—

Superstition is part of it, blooming where the tail leaves off, spreading out, fingers touching all the parts of my day. I'll sit in the doorway, too, if that will make time move backward, reattach what is lost. If it will help me find what I can now only vaguely remember.

Small Buddha

She is the girl next door. She is soft and sly and brilliant
and exuberant and demure. She and I eat oysters together,
and drink a little beer. We live on different sides of the
railroad tracks. But it is Mardi Gras, and we're both wearing beads around our necks tonight, and she gives me this
small red Buddha.

Color Chart

Black egg, black shirt, black Wyoming sky, blackout with
white lightning, blackout with snow, black TV in hotel at
night; brown eyes like pine trees (or so I wrote), molasses,
blackguard, his necklace, his knees; purple is an explosion,
in me; red quilt, nocturnal visits like some wanted crime
scene, red never fully, red as a destination; dark blue only
less vibrant, blue as the child's sweater and snap-up cow-
girl shirt, blue as my mother's underwear, squares of pale
nylon or silk such as girls don't wear nowadays or ever, blue
as the room in the château, the blue of imminent, the blue
of expansion, this blue, blue as her eyes, as the china left
by the dead; green this and that, green everything in the
book, why so much inordinate green? delete the green,
make the green toward, green of absence, green of never,
green of not anymore, green of fucked up bullshit, green
of complaint, green howling when it comes up out of nowhere on a road through little green, green of elsewhere,
and again; yellow funny dress photograph, fake look, fake
pearls, yellow tablecloth, yellow background for self-por-
trait, I can be here and not this, the pale yellow of my room,
the room I later painted, the room we painted together, the
other room, the room my parents painted, the lost rooms,
the complete; the taupe, the beige, the tan, khaki pants, my
boyfriend's pants, bargaining, me a tan clown in too-big
boots, the khaki of all that and the way it just disappeared
afterward like—; the white pretty; the white I wore to my
father's wedding, the white that is not at hospitals, the white

of the cat in the flame, the white of the page, the white surrounding my hands, the white when you can't see, the white that is black, the white folded, the white fallen away, the white surrounding the iris, the confusion of white, clustering, the white of an airplane ticket slipped into a black pocket, the white of the broken ocean and the white bunny; three other colors, pears, coins, drinks.

Density

Call the eighty-nine-year-old woman, your great aunt, at the new facility. The last time you called she'd broken down and told you how she hated it and how she'd had pretty much a nervous breakdown when she was packing up her things from her old home, where she'd lived for forty years, and there was no one to help her and she just started getting rid of it all, couldn't decide who to give what to. That last time was months ago. But you will call her now. It's a relatively calm Sunday. Laundry is done. No schoolwork today. And she's pretty nice. Call her. She's got one brother she doesn't see that often and she'll tell you today that he's broken his shoulder; she gets Communion but can't actually go to Mass and this bothers her, but she's glad for the Host, glad of that, anyway. Call her and—and remember the teacup she gave you, Irish, an ivy and shamrock pattern and the thinnest porcelain you can imagine, thinner with age, so delicate you can almost see through it, so delicate, so light, as light as a wing in your hand—call her and you don't have that much time, but you've been meaning to do it, you know it means something to her—so call her.

And say, "I'm sorry I didn't call earlier. It's been so long, I know. I've just been so busy."

"I know," she says, "everyone's busy. Isn't that the way it is though?"

Her voice is remote, though not unfriendly. Seize up anyway. Make it worse while you're at it. "I've heard that in America everyone really is a little busier (I just read that yesterday), but sometimes it just seems like it's a way we talk to each other, everyone has to be busier than the next person—"

"Yes," she says, a polite voice at the other end of the phone, from the nursing home. "Yes, sometimes it seems like an excuse."

"Yes," you say.

The conversation continues, as if no one has said anything.

Fire

Burning grain elevator across from his grandfather's train depot, the depot where Grandpa works and sleeps. Watching the flames from the car while his mother is elsewhere; his new winter parka. Yellow.

The hill is on fire, across the river. Later an explanation is given, something about the neighbor, a farmer. The cut of the horizon giving the fire definition, a place to begin.

Traveling with his family on the train from Doyon, North Dakota, through Minneapolis, to Chicago. Annual trip. In the middle of the night, waking up. Hurtling through flames for what seems like miles. A burn off of some kind. How close are they? If you pass your finger through flame—

Burns, a scar. A recollection confirmed by his mother. Stories told by candlelight on our daughter's first fishing trip. First memory, and they say the soul cannot be defined. I say otherwise, husband of fire.

AURELIE SHEEHAN

Police

Beyond the shopping center parking lot, above it, the sky has broken from the inside and a far too expansive, far greater than usual, almost embarrassing, divine or certainly orgasmic profusion of orange-pink rays stream out from a rift in the clouds. The clouds themselves are outlined with shimmering blue. The light has taken shape; it's got dimension and intent, a capacity for benediction. The shape is both ordered and disordered, a great mess on a canvas of sky. People have stopped and are staring. They hold onto their grocery carts as if to stop from falling, from fainting. Everything is slow motion and quiet. The night will not come. The sky just keeps getting bigger, the colors seeping out from whatever was behind. If you would panic, you would panic. If you would gasp, you would gasp. It is that amazing.

As my daughter and I watch the sky, eight or ten cops come out of the Mexican take-out restaurant and stride toward their motorcycles, parked in a cluster by the shopping cart corral. They do not slow down; they do not stop in the middle of the parking lot to gape. Perhaps one of them is looking up secretly as the others speak? Now they are gathering around their bikes, putting on gloves, helmets. Surely those two will stop, will point. Surely that one will. Surely this last one will take a look, will furtively stare at the glory, after the others have rumbled on and out of the parking lot—I would not think less of her if she did.

Paper Bag

Years later I tried to understand.

The freckles, the tipped ears, the sculpted forehead, eyes black as a well.

It made a remote kind of sense, light refracting on a September night, surely there's a reason for it: why this painfully beautiful sunset, why now for the god-shadows and the pregnant orange? Everybody loves somebody, I think that's what the poster said. Aquarius, Libra. Both from Detroit. I think it's chancier, the way somebody you're not even thinking about, you don't even like, shows up in a dream, sits in your mother's chair or writes in pen on the document. You're found. There's no way out.

He laid certain garments before me and asked me to choose. He had no scent, or should I say his scent was maddeningly distant. It was probably clear to all you people that he was the chosen one, that light danced on his shoulders as he walked the quarter mile to the store on the hill, came back with his paper bag: a gift for the cook. I inferred that he ate, slept, and shat like other humans from this planet, but from the first time I read the poems about roads and fire I couldn't believe he was like anyone else, that he was like me, a cat with a heart murmur, a bum with a limp.

At his funeral I am the one in back, a black shadow from central casting. I am the skeleton in a cloak, I am the throbbing red heart. It is a dream they shared, the relatives and friends and coworkers, a dream of feet on the ground, of a potato-chip bowl, of a casserole in the oven, of a brother-in-law just out of the shower, of a receipt from Target.

We live, I whisper. I can do that much. *We live*—out here, pure in heart, skeletal, barely understood.

Can you hear me? Will you ever hear me?

Let me spell it out.

Mermaid

At least half the time you have to share a lane; today is one of those days. Adult swimmers are traveling back and forth in a line, and then in the wide lane closest to the lockers an old woman is doing therapeutic movement. One of the people in the pool this morning, I realize, is a child. Highly unusual. Expressly forbidden.

She's about ten, I'd say. When I see that she's a child—it's more a sense of how she moves, rather than her facial features or her size—I choose another lane. I dip in, begin the first of two crawl laps (followed by breaststroke, then repeated four times).

The girl is not actually swimming. She's walking the line painted on the pool floor, balancing against the buoyancy of water. Eventually she just begins to meander. She links herself in various ways to the rope between her lane and mine, looking down into the water, diving underneath, and coming back up again. I am prepared mentally to swim my twelve laps, in a particular order, in unwavering succession. I have been doing this for about twenty years, as crazy as that sounds. I never deviate, never stop or slow down.

The girl is looking at me often, I can tell that in my peripheral vision, a face turned in my direction. Then she begins to race me for half a lap. I see her thrashing, I hear her breath. She is tampering with the linearity of my morning! I plunge forward, keep going.

But at the same time I've newly noticed the sunlight

coming in from the vast picture windows, all the blue, all the bleached white. On my tenth turn, I pop up from the water, see that she's at the wall, too. "Hi," I say, in her general direction. Through my goggles, I see her face break into a wide smile. "Hi," she says back, her voice friendly, young, ready to play. She is curious about the other side.

Tooth

A piece of fabric laid out, and a selection of tools. Outdoors, by the road, near the other vendors. The man hawks as all hawkers hawk. He promises, cajoles, lures, relieves. Tooth pain is everything. You pay first. It's still a lot to pay, but you can afford this treatment. Well, there's almost no choice. You sit on the small piece of red fabric and he picks up one of the tools: the chisel. You open your mouth. Into your mouth go the chisel and the hacksaw. Into your mouth goes the ice pick. The man distracts you with a comment, and then he applies fast, intense pressure until the browning tooth cracks. Around you the sky means something, anything. Your heart is hard, and then it expands.

Acknowledgments

With thanks to the editors of the journals where these pieces originally appeared, especially first responders Drew Burk and Richard Siken of *Spork*, and Sam Ligon of *Willow Springs*.

Alice Redux: New Stories of Alice, Lewis and Wonderland: "Book" [as "Tumble"];
Blackbird: "Pillbox";
Cutthroat: "Purse";
Guernica: A Magazine of Art & Politics: "Big Truck," "Pain";
Gulf Coast: "Ambition," "Devotion," "Dishes the Cat Used, Now Stored in the Laundry Room";
Hotel Amerika: "Paper Bag";
Quick Fiction: "Mermaid";
Sonora Review: "A Liar and Her Brother," "Density," "Glass," "Gun," "Police," "Stone";
The Southern Review: "Cup of Coffee," "Jewelry Box," "Letters," "Small Buddha," "Telephone Call," "Wallet";
Spork: "Age at Which You Consider History," "Artists," "Boat," "Color Chart," "Daughter," "Hair," "Joke," "Kleenex Box," "Mascara," "Motherhood," "Mushroom Paté," "Rabbits," "Rage," "Sexual Fantasy," "Talk," "Tooth";
Willow Springs: "Boots," "Bratz Doll," "Cigarette," "Kitchen," "Shoes," "Story," "Suntan Lotion," "T-shirt";
Writing as Revision: "Mascara," "Purse."

I am grateful to all my readers, including Beth Alvarado, Kate Bernheimer, Lydia Millet, Ander Monson, Stacey Richter, Frederic Tuten, Joshua Marie Wilkinson, and Jason Zuzga. Enduring thanks to the love of my life, an editor and writer without equal, Reed Karaim.

About the Author

Aurelie Sheehan is the author of two novels, *History Lesson for Girls* and *The Anxiety of Everyday Objects*, as well as a short story collection, *Jack Kerouac Is Pregnant*. Her work has appeared in many venues including *Alaska Quarterly Review*, *Conjunctions*, *Epoch*, *Fairy Tale Review*, *Fence*, *New England Review*, *The New York Times*, *Ploughshares*, and *The Southern Review*. She has received a Pushcart Prize, a Camargo Fellowship, the Jack Kerouac Literary Award, and an Artist Project Grant from the Arizona Commission on the Arts. Sheehan teaches in the MFA program at the University of Arizona in Tucson.

BOA Editions, Ltd. American Reader Series

Colophon

BOA Editions, Ltd., a not-for-profit publisher of poetry and other literary works, fosters readership and appreciation of contemporary literature. By identifying, cultivating, and publishing both new and established poets and selecting authors of unique literary talent, BOA brings high-quality literature to the public. Support for this effort comes from the sale of its publications, grant funding, and private donations.

The publication of this book is made possible, in part, by the special support of the following individuals:

Anonymous
Bernadette Catalana
Anne Germanacos
Robert & Willy Hursh
X. J. & Dorothy M. Kennedy
Katy Lederer
Boo Poulin
Steve O. Russell & Phyllis Rifkin-Russell